"You're embarassed. Why?"

When she didn't answer, Mitch smiled and gave her hand a brief squeeze. "What's to be embarassed about?"

"You didn't fall down the stairs in front of a stranger," Jamie replied, chagrined.

"Neither did you. You'd already fallen when I came in," he teased.

"You're splitting hairs," she said, trying to disengage her hand. "Besides, I imagine you're used to women falling at your feet."

"Now, why would you say a thing like that?"

"Are you trying to say there isn't any truth to those stories about you and all those women?" Jamie asked him in an incredulous tone.

"Are you trying to say you care if there is or not?" he retaliated.

Dear Reader,

Sophisticated but sensitive, savvy yet unabashedly sentimental—that's today's woman, today's romance reader—you! And Silhouette Special Editions are written expressly to reward your quest for substantial, emotionally involving love stories.

So take a leisurely stroll under the cover's lavender arch into a garden of romantic delights. Pick and choose among titles if you must—we hope you'll soon equate all six Special Editions each month with consistently gratifying romantic reading.

Watch for sparkling new stories from your Silhouette favorites—Nora Roberts, Tracy Sinclair, Ginna Gray, Lindsay McKenna, Curtiss Ann Matlock, among others—along with some exciting newcomers to Silhouette, such as Karen Keast and Patricia Coughlin. Be on the lookout, too, for the new Silhouette Classics, a distinctive collection of bestselling Special Editions and Silhouette Intimate Moments now brought back to the stands—two each month—by popular demand.

On behalf of all the authors and editors of Special Editions,
Warmest wishes,

Leslie Kazanjian
Senior Editor

BAY
MATTHEWS
Lessons
in Loving

Silhouette Special Edition

Published by Silhouette Books New York

America's Publisher of Contemporary Romance

For Jo Lu and Roger with love and thanks.
Special thanks to Darlene Pace,
a teacher with vision
and to Janet Singleton and all the teachers
of special education for their love and caring.

SILHOUETTE BOOKS
300 East 42nd St., New York, N.Y. 10017

Copyright © 1987 by Penny Richards

ISBN: 0-373-09420-5

First Silhouette Books printing November 1987

America's Publisher of Contemporary Romance

Printed in the U.S.A.

Books by Bay Matthews

Silhouette Special Edition

Bittersweet Sacrifice #298
Roses and Regrets #347
Some Warm Hunger #391
Lessons in Loving #420

BAY MATTHEWS

of Haughton, LA, describes herself as a dreamer and an incurable romantic. Married at an early age to her high school sweetheart, she claims she grew up with her three children. Now that only the youngest is at home, writing romances adds a new dimension to the already exciting life she leads on her husband's Thoroughbred farm.

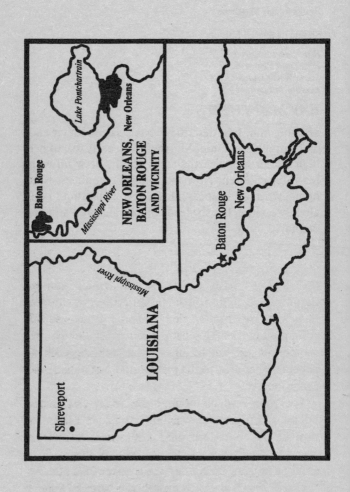

Chapter One

The sounds of children at play penetrated the windows protecting the warmth of the schoolroom from the unusually bitter cold of a late January day in Baton Rouge, falling on Jamie Carr's ears as a muted hum. One particularly piercing shriek splintered off from the rest, breaking her concentration, which was sporadic at best, and lifting her gaze from the stack of papers on her desk to the playground just outside the classroom.

The room, which housed the usual elementary school accoutrements, was also filled with Jamie's own brand of motivational stimulants. A bulletin board with a Shel Silverstein drawing of two smiling children hugging each other and a copy of his famous "Hug O' War" poem. A poster of a battered knight riding a tired-looking steed and carrying a broken lance and a banner proclaiming I Can. A table purposely left scattered with construction paper, roundnosed scissors and glue, plus a veritable rainbow of crayons, colored pencils and felt-tip markers. A popcorn popper. Multi-hued fabric swatches. A tape player. Paper snowflakes sprinkled with iridescent glitter—each different, unique.

Color. Texture.

A gold mine in contrasts to please the eye and sharpen the senses and the mind.

Ignoring her surroundings, Jamie rested her chin in the cradle of her hands, her slim, ringless fingers framing her lightly freckled face. Her green eyes watched the romping children without really seeing them. Her dark eyebrows were furrowed in a frown, and she chewed her lower lip in contemplation while one finger twisted a lock of almost-black hair around and around.

"Hey!" came a cheerful and familiar voice from the doorway. "What's the matter with you? Did one of the kids accidentally squish Lester?"

Jamie turned toward her friend and fellow teacher, Leah Jeffries. A smile kicked up the corners of her mouth at the woman's mention of Lester, the somewhat child-shocked resident chameleon. "Lester's fine," she said. "What are you doing here?"

"My free period," Leah said around a mouthful of apple.

Jamie cast a quick glance at the large clock on the far wall. "Good grief! I can't believe how the day has gotten away from me. Recess will be over in five minutes."

"Speaking of which, why aren't you outside?" Leah asked.

"I have playground duty next week. Maybe it'll warm up some by then," Jamie said hopefully, gathering up the papers and placing them on a pile of folders. She reached for her coffee cup and hit the papers with her elbow. The entire stack slithered to the floor, drawing a mild oath from Jamie and a smile from Leah.

"Maybe," Leah said. "So what are you so glum about?"

Jamie grew pensive again. "It's been almost two weeks since he's been gone." She spoke as if Leah knew exactly who "he" was.

Pushing aside a pencil holder with the Special Olympics logo on its side, Leah perched on the one vacant corner of Jamie's desk. "He, who?" she asked before taking another bite of her apple.

Jamie frowned up into her friend's curious brown eyes. "Chris Decker." When Leah continued to look down at her with the extreme patience reserved for the very young or the very dense, Jamie realized Leah wasn't a mind reader and added, "The child whose parents were killed in the private plane crash a few weeks ago."

Recognition dawned on Leah's pretty, plump face. "Oh, yeah, I remember. Maybe he's just having a hard time adjusting."

Jamie gave a deep sigh. "According to your husband, our illustrious principal, the office was just informed that Chris probably wouldn't be back to school at all."

"What?" Leah said. "But Chris has to go to school."

Jamie shrugged. "It seems he's in the custody of his uncle, who's waiting for an opening to get Chris into Barstow. In the meantime, he's having him tutored."

"It must be nice," Leah commented dryly, clearly unimpressed by the private boarding school's name.

"Yeah. The sad thing is that Chris loves school." Jamie's eyes flashed with irritation. "He *needs* school, for crying out loud! If you ask me, it's a cop-out. The man just doesn't want to be bothered with a kid like Chris."

Leah's expression softened with understanding. "You're worried about what will happen to Chris with his parents gone and him getting stuck in a place where no one really loves him."

"Yes," Jamie said firmly, "I am. Joyce and Michael Decker were wonderful parents, wonderful people. The fact that their only child was mentally handicapped didn't lessen their love for him one bit."

"Who is his uncle anyway?"

"Joyce Decker's brother, Mitchell Bishop, former football player and owner of Bishop's Sporting Goods. From what Sam says, that's who informed him Chris wouldn't be back."

Leah whistled. Mitchell Bishop was something of a legend in Louisiana—a lower middle class kid who'd made it big as a major league quarterback, then been cut down in his glory years by a rash of serious injuries. Undaunted, Bishop had taken his name and a substantial amount of borrowed money, his considerable charm and a lot of guts, and bought a floundering Chicago sporting goods manufacturing firm. The rest was history.

"Do you think Chris is in his care permanently?"

Jamie twisted a single spiral curl around her index finger. "Who knows? It's probably only temporary custody."

"Why do you say that?"

With a look that was a twin to the patience in Leah's face only seconds before, Jamie said, "C'mon, Leah. You know as well as I do that it takes a special person to cope with kids like Chris, and if the gossip mill is on target with the quantity of women in his life, being responsible for any kid will cramp Mitchell Bishop's style."

"Yeah," Leah said with a dreamy sigh. "He is a hunk, isn't he?"

Jamie leaned back in her chair and rolled her eyes toward the acoustical-tile ceiling. "Leah, please."

"What?" her friend asked with round-eyed innocence.

"Try not to salivate on my reports."

Leah, who had been happily married to Sam Jeffries for eleven years, giggled. "Look, kiddo, I may be married, I may be a mother, but I ain't dead yet. Don't tell me you never noticed how handsome he is."

Jamie took a swallow of her cooling coffee, propped her chin in her hand and stared at her friend in a way that asked if she'd just lost her mind.

"It isn't fair to judge them all because you got a bad one," Leah reminded her.

"Two bad ones," Jamie corrected. "And in all fairness to those two jerks, what happened was as much my fault as theirs."

"It was?"

"Sure. My brother always said that no one will walk on you until you lie down and let him."

Leah regarded Jamie thoughtfully. "I just can't picture you letting anyone take advantage."

"Youth," Jamie said. "Youth and illusions."

Before Leah could comment, a bell clanged in the hallway. Jamie dropped her head into her hands with a moan. "Back to the salt mines."

"Don't give me that," Leah said, sliding from the corner of the desk and straightening her sweater over her ample hips. "Everyone knows you love what you do, which is why you're so good at it."

"Leah..."

"I know. I know. You hate praise." She tossed her apple core into the trashcan and licked her fingers. "Do you think Sam could talk Bishop into letting Chris come back?"

The noise Jamie made sounded suspiciously like a snort. "Are you kidding? Sam is tops as principals go, but he can't personally involve himself in the lives of fifteen hundred students."

Leah cocked her head consideringly. "True. So what are you going to do?"

Jamie's eyes were bleak as she confessed, "I don't know, but I'll think of something."

Jamie was still pondering what to do about Chris late that afternoon when the last child had been ushered to the bus, when her desk was straight and when the door to her room had been locked carefully behind her. Her question remained unanswered as she drove to her apartment, the same apartment she'd moved to five years earlier when her husband had informed her that her—as he put it—"ingenue" look just wouldn't cut it as the proper image for his wife.

As the brains and drive behind Image Makers, one of the newest and fastest growing publicity agencies in the country, which handled some of the best-known authors and politicians around, Chad felt he had his own image to maintain. Unfortunately for Jamie, his image demanded a wife who was sophisticated, savvy, chic and looked like a model—not a twenty-three-year-old woman who wore faded jeans and looked all of eighteen. Also unfortunately for Jamie, Shelly, his first wife, with her model-slim figure and cover-girl face, wanted to come back, and Jamie had to admit there was certainly nothing wrong with Shelly's image.

She sighed at the memories and pulled into her regular parking space. Clutching the key ring in her teeth and gathering her usual stack of papers, she bumped the door to her red CRX shut with a swing of her hip, headed for the front door, unlocked it and stepped inside with a sigh of relief.

Though it had been one of the first apartment complexes built in the area five years ago and was so far out of the city that many Baton Rouge residents felt it was too far to drive, Jamie had loved its semi-seclusion. But the inevitable growth of Baton Rouge had edged the city limits closer and closer. Now there was a shopping center just up the street and a convenience store on every corner.

The complex itself was still well maintained, and the rooms were spacious. The downstairs consisted of a kitchen large enough for a small table, a combined

living and dining room and a half bath off the entrance hall. French doors led to a patio and over-
looked a hanky-size backyard with a bird bath
surrounded by some rocks she'd carefully chosen from
her grandmother's farm in Arkansas.

Dragging her jacket up the stairs to her bedroom,
Jamie kicked off her fleece-lined high-heeled boots
and slipped her feet into furry house slippers de-
signed to look like bear paws, complete with toenails.
Her brother, who had bought them as a gag gift for
Christmas, couldn't believe she actually wore them.
But, Jamie told him, they *were* warm, and she hated
to be cold, so why not?

Padding back downstairs, she made herself a cup of
hot chocolate and a peanut butter sandwich and ate it
standing at the patio doors, watching a variety of birds
fight over the seed in the feeder and the stealthy stalk-
ing of a neighborhood cat who slunk from rock to
rock, just waiting to pounce. Like the cat, dusk
crouched behind each corner and tree, waiting to
snatch the last remaining bit of day. A sudden gust of
wind sent a flurry of leaves tumbling across the yard,
scattering the birds and sending a shiver down Jamie's spine.

She took a warming sip of the hot drink and turned
back to the room. She couldn't believe she wouldn't
have Chris in school anymore. It was funny how there
was a special child in every class. It had been that way
before she'd gone into special education, and she'd
soon found that it was the same there. Chris Decker
had been this year's child, the one who brought
laughter to her lips and tugged at her heartstrings.

With heaviness weighing down her usually high spirits, she finished her sandwich and forced herself back upstairs to the extra bedroom she had converted into an office.

Two hours later she finished the drawing of a clown she would photocopy for the children to color the next day, pleased with the jauntiness of his costume and the curve of his smile. With a sigh of satisfaction, she went to the bathroom and submerged all but her head in a super-hot bubble bath that was guaranteed to ease tensions and drive away the chill.

Her conversation with Leah played through her mind like the lyrics of a song that wouldn't leave her alone.

"Do you think Sam could talk Bishop into letting Chris come back?"

No. It wasn't Sam's place, Jamie reasoned.

Then whose place was it?

Mine, she realized.

"So what are you going to do?"

The questions and answers raced through her mind, coming out of left field, coming out of the knowledge that somebody had to do something. She sat up suddenly in the tub, the water and iridescent bubbles sluicing down her body in a cascade.

Why hadn't she thought of it sooner? She was the logical person to intervene with Mitchell Bishop. She was the one who knew what was best for Chris, and the last thing he needed right now was to be yanked out of his familiar routine, away from faces he knew, and put into a private school simply to get him out of his uncle's hair!

Once the idea was fully formed, there was no turning back. Impulsive action was no stranger to Jamie; she had always been a doer. Clumsy with impatience, she dragged the bobby pins from her hair and anchored the sides back with combs. Not bothering with makeup, she tugged on snug, wash-softened jeans and a long, floppy sweater. With growing agitation she covered the ensemble with a full-length coat of snow-white Tibetan lamb she'd bought for its warmth the winter before in spite of the price that was a death-blow to her ailing savings account.

Setting a royal-blue beret on her hair and pulling on matching gloves, she bounded down the stairs. She snatched her keys from the glass-topped coffee table and raced out into the winter night, the cold and the lure of challenge making her breathless with exhilaration.

The wind blowing outside rattled the shutters and howled through the night. Shrubs scratched the side of the house like fingernails against a chalkboard. Mitch Bishop rubbed his aching knee and moved instinctively toward the fireplace, even though the Victorian house he called home was far from cold. Placing one Gucci-shod foot on the raised hearth, he rested his forearm on his bent knee and leaned toward the flames, a squat glass of Chivas Regal clenched in square, strong fingers. He absentmindedly stroked his stubbled jaw, then ran a restless hand through his coffee-brown hair. His eyes, brown and serious, regarded the dancing flames, searching for answers to his question of Why? and coming up empty-handed.

He swirled the caramel-hued liquid in his glass, hardly noticing when it sloshed over the side. It seemed impossible that less than three weeks ago his sister, Joyce, and her husband, Michael, had laughed with him in this very room as they tried to talk him into asking out Michael's new secretary. Finding her brother a "good wife" had been one of Joyce's self-appointed goals in life. But now, thanks to a malfunction in the engine of their small plane, Joyce and Michael would never laugh in this room again. The secretary was out of a job. And Joyce would never find him a wife.

Tears, hot and stinging, flooded his eyes. Anger at the unfairness of life and a frustration that was devouring him from the inside out made Mitch down a choking mouthful of the whiskey. He grimaced and tossed the remaining liquor onto the burning logs. The fire hissed as it consumed the alcohol and belched up a roaring flame.

He recoiled from the suddenly intense heat and turned back to the elegance of the room. Roughly eighteen by eighteen, the library, like the rest of the house, boasted ceilings that an energy management team had begged him to lower. Floor-to-ceiling bookcases on one wall were balanced on the opposite wall by the fireplace flanked by more shelves filled with everything from books to bric-a-brac to samples of the equipment he manufactured. A sleek football on a pedestal, a gleaming helmet, shoulder pads elegant in their rugged simplicity—all were stamped with white block letters spelling *Bishop*, a name synonymous with quality, all proclaiming him a success by anyone's standards.

Mitch moved to the massive walnut desk near one of the room's huge windows. Placing the empty glass on the gleaming surface with no regard for its fine patina, he pulled out the chair and lowered himself into the worn leather, stretching his bad leg out in an effort to ease the pain. The chair creaked with his weight, a comforting, familiar sound. God knew he needed some comfort, some familiarity, now that his whole life was changed...now that he had Chris to raise.

As if on cue, a small, slightly plump boy with light brown hair that fell over his forehead came running into the room. A puffing, grandmotherly looking woman followed close behind him.

"No bed!"

The emphatic words vibrated from the eight-year-old, who stood with his feet apart and his arms folded belligerently across his chest. They were accompanied by a negative shake of his head, a downturned mouth and defiant blue eyes.

Filled, as usual, by a feeling of total uncertainty as how best to handle the situation, Mitch regarded the stubbornness in the set of his nephew's round chin.

"C'mon, Chris," he said with what he hoped was an encouraging smile. "You've got to go take your bath and get ready for bed."

Chris offered his uncle another vigorous shake of his head and a gesture that mimicked an umpire designating a runner safe. "No me."

Mattie Henley, the fifty-four-year-old widow Mitch had hired to look after Chris, gave a shake of her graying head and said, "You'd better get into that bathroom, Chris Decker. Now!"

Chris stood firmly in place, looking at her out of the corner of his eye. Seeing no compromise there, he dropped his arms to his sides and began to sidle toward Mitch. "Go Mama house," he said, looking up at Mitch with a gleam in his eyes that signaled the gathering of tears.

"You can't go to Mama's house, Chris," Mitch said.

"Hy?" he asked, unable to pronounce the W.

Mitch's feeble bid for control tumbled beneath the weight of the single word. Chris had an uncanny ability to disarm him with a word or a look. He glanced at the sitter, who looked back helplessly.

Mitch sighed and said the first thing that came to mind. "Because Mama isn't there right now."

Chris's shoulders slumped with a sadness he couldn't vocalize, and his forehead wrinkled beneath the fringe of his bangs. "Hy?"

Mitch's panic-laden gaze flew to Mattie's again. The heart-wrenching question enlarged the lump in his throat. His eyes closed, a barrier against the threatening tears. The tears were stopped, but he couldn't stop the pictures of the funeral that flashed through his mind like slides in a carousel. How could he explain the loss of Joyce and Michael to Chris? How much would the boy even understand? Dear heaven, what could he say? How did you explain death to any child, especially one with Down's syndrome?

Mattie Henley intervened. She placed a gentle hand on Chris's shoulder and said, "She just isn't there right now, Chris. Come on, like a good boy, and let's take our bath. I'll get you some cocoa and a cookie before you go to bed."

The change in Chris was instantaneous. A smile lifted his round cheeks. His slightly slanted eyes no longer held a touch of hurt but twinkled with new happiness. He rubbed his palms together with glee. "Okay!"

He sped from the room and down the hall.

Mitch offered the woman a relieved smile. "Thanks."

She nodded, and Mitch watched as she left the room. His momentary relief crumpled beneath the weight of despair that sent his elbows to the desktop and the fingers of both hands plowing through his hair. What, he wondered with panic, did a single man do when he was suddenly responsible for an eight-year-old boy who was mentally handicapped?

Even though Joyce and Michael had both been past prime child-rearing age, they had made parenting Chris look like a breeze. But Mitch was learning quickly that it wasn't a breeze. It was hard. Maybe the hardest thing he'd ever undertaken in his life.

You could put him in the state school and never have to worry about him again... The voices of well-meaning friends came back to taunt him.

"No!" His vocal response to the mind-whispered temptation was instant and emphatic. It echoed loudly through the silence of the empty room. No matter how hard things got for him, he wouldn't do that. Joyce would never forgive him. He'd never forgive himself.

Twelve years older than he, Mitch's sister had always wanted a baby. She and Michael had tried all their married life to have one, but life had denied them until it was ready, and Joyce had been forty-one by then. Forty-one with all the odds stacked against her.

Anemia. Rh factor. Age. It had been doubly hard when, in her fourth month of pregnancy, amniocentesis revealed a problem, and they were faced with the knowledge that the child they'd longed for, dreamed of and prayed for would be born with Down's syndrome.

Abortion, of course, was out of the question. It had amazed Mitch to see both Joyce and Michael grieve, then put their sorrow aside and go on as if nothing were out of the ordinary and everything was fine. Chris's birth had been met with all the joy that would have greeted any normal, long-awaited child. He had been welcomed into the world by parents who loved him, parents who were determined to do their best by him.

Mitch swallowed hard and clenched his fingers in his hair. He wanted to do his best by Chris, and personal experience had taught him that people could be cruel when they didn't understand. He wanted to shelter the child, to keep people from hurting him the way he'd been hurt. But dealing with Chris was out of his realm of expertise. It was hard to know what to do day after day, for the rest of both their lives.

Something clicked unexpectedly in his mind. Something he had refused until now to face, but something he must face in order to do his best for Chris. That something was the fact that unlike other children, children who had problems with schoolwork, grades, trouble in class—even drinking or drugs—Chris wouldn't grow up and leave home. Chris was forever....

The doorbell rang, jerking Mitch's eyes open and shattering the moment of revelation. He shoved back the cuff of his tailored shirt just as the grandfather clock down the hall began to strike the hour. The gold Rolex nestled against the dark hair on his wrist read eight o'clock. Who would be visiting at this hour? The bell rang again, and he remembered that Mrs. Henley was getting Chris ready for bed. He'd have to answer the door himself.

Pushing himself away from the desk as the bell chimed a third time, he crossed the plush carpet and stepped into the hall, limping slightly on his bad leg. His heels clicked briefly on aged oak planks before the sound of his footsteps was swallowed by the Turkish rug sheltering the gleaming hardwood.

He flipped on the outside lights, shot back the bolt and opened the door. Frigid wind rushed into the room uninvited, and Mitch's gaze found a woman standing bathed in the porch's light.

His overall impression was of vitality and youth, a shaggy white coat and curly black hair. Probably a teenager collecting for something or other for school. Or maybe she needed to use the phone.

During the scant instant it took for him to absorb her presence, she licked her lips and, for some unknown reason, took a step backward. The wind whipped white spirals of wool and black spirals of hair across the moistness of her mouth. Desire—unexpected, sharp and entirely out of place—knifed through him.

Mitch cursed himself mentally and shifted his gaze from her mouth to her eyes, eyes that some part of his mind registered were much older than her image suggested. But before he recognized that fact fully, he heard himself say, "Hi, honey. What can I do for you?"

"Mr. Bishop?"

Mitch noticed that, for some inexplicable reason, her eyes had cooled to the color of freezing ocean spray, and, if possible, her voice was a few degrees colder than her eyes. For the life of him he didn't know what had happened. His heavy eyebrows drew together in a frown. "Yes?"

"I'm Jamie Carr, Chris's teacher. May I come in?"

Chapter Two

Chris's teacher?" Mitch could hear the incredulity in his voice even as he wondered *what* teacher. "But you don't look..."

"Old enough," Jamie finished for him, barely able to keep from gnashing her teeth in disgust.

"Right."

"I'd like to talk to you for a few minutes, if I may."

"Oh. Sure," he said, making no effort to let her in.

Jamie stared up into the surprise on his face while the cold wind swirled around them. Her dark eyebrows rose in question. "May I come in?"

"Oh, sure," Mitch said again, moving aside for her to enter and wondering if her incredibly long eyelashes were real.

Stepping into the comparative warmth of the foyer, Jamie peeled off her gloves and stuffed them into her pockets while her gaze roamed the hallway. The central heating system kicked on at the same time the door clicked shut, no doubt in response to the invasion of wintry cold.

"Let me take your coat," Mitch offered, moving behind her and placing his hands on her shoulders. She was tall, her forehead on a line with his mouth, and slight beneath the bulky coat.

He drew in a shallow breath, and his senses were assaulted with a clean, light fragrance that drifted from her, undulating upward on the draft of warm air blowing from the vents in the baseboards. Shampoo? Perfume? The scent brought to mind nostalgic memories of sunny days, line-dried sheets and problem-free springtimes.

Making a visible effort to bring himself back to the present, Mitch helped her from the furry covering and hung it on a brass hook of the antique hall tree that graced one wainscoted wall. When he turned back, she was contemplating the turned railings of the staircase and pushing up the sleeves of the oversized cowl-neck sweater that hit her at the middle of her denim-covered thighs. As far as he could tell in the bulky outfit, he'd been right. She was slender.

She tucked a lock of curly, nearly black shoulder-length hair behind a small ear that bore a single pearl stud and crossed her arms as if she were cold, an action that emphasized the curve of her breasts. Then her wandering gaze meandered back to his and locked for interminable, animosity-filled seconds.

Mitch wondered what he'd done to deserve her attitude. He started to ask—and not politely—but remembered just in time that she was there about Chris.

Maybe he'd better play it by ear for a while longer. The decision brought back the keen sense of objectivity that had helped get him where he was in the world. He felt his control, a control he'd somehow lost when he saw her standing in the doorway a minute before, return. Smiling the wide white smile that generated a dimple in his left cheek, Mitch said, "Let's go into the library."

He indicated the door with a sweep of his hand and followed her into the room, liking the slight sway of her hips beneath the long sweater. Liking it very much. He shook his head. He still couldn't believe she was old enough to be teaching. And he couldn't understand his reaction to this youthful wraith. Cradlerobbing had never been his thing.

"Would you like something to drink?" he asked once she was seated in one of the wing chairs before the fireplace.

"No, thank you."

He almost shivered at the coolness frosting her voice... and fixed himself another Chivas Regal. Something told him he would need it.

Drink in hand, he sat down in the opposite chair and crossed his legs, reaching out in an automatic gesture to massage his bad knee.

"So you're from Barstow?" he asked at last.

At his mention of the private school where he hoped to put Chris, Jamie frowned. "Whatever gave you that idea? I work with the public school system."

Mitch's confusion was apparent. "But I've taken Chris out of public school. I'm having him tutored until there's an opening at Barstow."

"I know, Mr. Bishop. That's why I'm here. I'd like to ask you to reconsider sending Chris to a private school—especially a boarding school."

The motion of Mitch's hand stopped. Part of him wanted to demand if it were any of her business; part of him was intrigued enough to ask, "Why?"

"Because at this point in his life, Chris needs familiarity. If you send him away to school, you'll be doing him a terrible injustice."

"Barstow has an excellent reputation," he reminded her.

"Chris needs *you*, right now, Mr. Bishop," she said earnestly, "not a school's reputation. Not the anonymity he'll get in Barstow."

"Look, I appreciate your concern, but I'm a busy man, Miss Carr, and—"

"Ms.," she supplied.

Mitch's smile was thin. "Of course, *Ms.* Carr. I really feel this is the best thing for Chris. I travel a lot, and it will be easier all around if Chris could get settled into some sort of routine. Barstow is perfect."

Disbelief—or was it disdain—filled her eyes. "Mr. Bishop, Chris Decker just lost his parents."

Mitch's control of his temper slipped a millimeter in the face of her tenacity. His brown eyes speared hers. "I am well aware of that fact, Ms. Carr. Joyce Decker was my sister."

"And her death hurt you?"

Mitch uncrossed his legs and leaned toward her, resting his forearms on his knees. "What the hell kind of question is that? Of course, it hurt me."

"And don't you think Chris suffered that hurt, as well?"

An uncomfortable feeling edged aside his anger. His eyes shifted from hers. "I don't think Chris understands exactly what happened."

"Have you told him?"

"How can I explain it to him?" he asked, snatching up his drink in sudden agitation. He stood and plunged his empty hand into his pocket, splaying the dark gray fabric across the most masculine part of him in a way Jamie found hard to ignore, even in her anger.

"What's the matter, Mr. Bishop?" she prodded. "Don't you think he deserves an explanation? Or don't you think he has the mentality to grasp it?"

Mitch moved in front of her so fast that Jamie had a sudden understanding of why he'd been such a success on the football field. She had to tip her head back to meet his brown eyes. His furious brown eyes.

A musky, masculine cologne, potent and sexy, enveloped her. He was so close that she could see the sherry-hued tints in his eyes and the faint lines etched by life and pain that rayed from their corners.

"You're way outta line, lady," he snarled softly down at her. He was fully aware that his own actions were out of line, too, but her comment, so close to the truth, brought a resurgence of his guilt, which was fed by his frustrating ignorance about how to cope with telling Chris. Unwilling to give in to the guilt, he waved his glass in the direction of the door and said, "I'm not interested in your opinions, so why don't you just haul your pretty little tail outta here?"

"I assure you, Mr. Bishop," she enunciated softly, "that I'd like nothing better, but I'm here because I'm concerned about Chris."

Mitch's eyes narrowed in consideration. He admired her style. She was furious, but she was being very careful not to let that anger get away from her. If it weren't for the stubborn tilt of her chin and the green sparks shooting from her eyes, you'd think, from listening to her tone of voice, that she was talking about something as innocuous as the weather. He had to give her credit for her conviction, even though Chris was really none of her business.

He forced a tight smile. "Don't be concerned, Ms. Carr. I'm taking excellent care of my nephew. He has a nice home, good food, an excellent sitter and a first-class tutor. What else could he possibly need?"

"How about love?"

The question hit him like the slap of a wet washcloth. The guts it took for her even to ask it was phenomenal. Fury—the likes of which he hadn't felt since the doctors told him he'd never play football again—rushed through Mitch with the speed of sound. He gripped the glass and downed a huge mouthful of the fiery liquid. The fact that he didn't choke or sputter was testimony to the degree of his anger. Carefully, as though it were a priceless piece of Ming, he set down the glass and counted to ten, struggling for rapidly deteriorating control.

Which turned out to be a waste of time.

Fury in every line of his face, he leaned over and grasped the soft flesh of Jamie's upper arm. Her startled gaze flew to his, and Mitch found himself sinking into eyes a deep, woodlands green flecked with brown and gold. He'd never seen such eyes. And the eyelashes were real. Definitely. He drew in a breath, and the smell of sunshine pricked his nostrils. Ignoring the pull on his senses, he exerted the slightest pressure upward on her arm and said in a voice of deadly calm, "As I said, Ms. Carr, why don't you just haul—"

"Ready bed, Mitz!"

Chris, his damp hair parted on the side and slicked back over his ears, barreled into the room. He was wearing flannel pajamas and a wide smile. His running steps and the smile both faltered when he saw that his uncle wasn't alone. His brown eyes shifted from Mitch to Jamie. Then the smile returned, wider and brighter than before. He ran toward her, his arms outstretched. "Miz Carr!"

Surprised by the happiness manifested in Chris's smile, Mitch released Jamie's arm and stepped aside. She dropped to her knees without the slightest hesitation and caught Chris as he flew into her arms.

Chris hugged Jamie, then leaned back and took her face between his pudgy hands, beaming and patting her cheek. "Where go?" he asked.

"Do you mean, where have I been?" she asked. When he nodded, she replied, "I've been working."

"'Cool?"

"Yes, Chris. At school."

Chris gave a thumbs-up sign with his right hand and nodded. Turning to Mitch, he said, "Me go 'cool!"

Jamie risked a glance at Mitch. The expression in his brown eyes was unreadable.

Actually, Mitch was trying to absorb the difference Chris's entrance had made in Jamie. Gone was the cold woman who'd questioned his love for Chris, and in her place was a warm, caring person whose own love for the boy couldn't be doubted.

Sensing that he no longer had her full attention, Chris turned Jamie's face back toward him, breaking the eye contact between her and Mitch. "Where Bo?"

Beau Parker was another of Jamie's students and Chris's best friend. She smiled. "Beau's at home. Probably in bed, where you should be."

"No me!" Chris said emphatically.

Mitch gave an inward groan. Did they have to go through all this again?

Jamie smiled and leaned her forehead against Chris's. "Ye-es, you-ou," she said in a singsong voice.

Chris smiled back and rubbed his short pug nose against hers. "No-o me-ee," he responded again, mimicking her to a T.

"Don't forget your hot chocolate," Mattie Henley reminded the boy from the doorway.

Chris pulled back and rubbed his stomach. "Mmmm." He cocked his thumb at Jamie and asked, "You?"

"No, thanks. I had some before I came. You go on and have yours."

"Awwight," Chris said. When he got to the doorway he faced the room briefly once more. "'Night, Miz Carr."

"Good night, Chris."

When he was gone, Jamie straightened up, the smile still on her face. Mitch thought it was probably one of the prettiest smiles he'd ever seen, a smile that spoke of caring and commitment.

"He really likes you," he told her with the barest hint of wonder in his voice.

Jamie turned. "I like him, too." The defensive tone she'd used earlier was gone. Her voice was as soft as the expression in her eyes. "That's what I was trying to get across to you, Mr. Bishop. Even though Chris doesn't know exactly where his parents are, he knows he no longer has their love around him. That's why he needs you and your love and familiar faces and places."

Mitch was silent.

Jamie offered him a slight smile. "I'm not denying that Barstow is a good school. I'm just saying that I don't think Chris will be happy there right now. And if you love him, his happiness should come first and foremost."

"At the risk of sounding callous, Ms. Carr, I do have a business to run."

"At the risk of beating a dead horse, Mr. Bishop, can't you delegate some of your duties?"

"No, Ms. Carr, I can't." He held a raised fist toward her. "Do you see this?"

Before Jamie could register the fact that the ring he meant was more than gold and diamonds, he said, "It's my Super Bowl ring."

Her eyes showed her puzzlement over how the ring could possibly be connected with the issue of Chris.

"I got it for the last game I played. That year I made it to the final game of the playoffs without getting hurt. I'd already had knee surgery twice." He stared across the room, memory shining in his eyes. "I had a great line, but even the best line can't cover you all the time. During the fourth quarter I wound up with about ten guys on top of my bum knee.

"The coaches and the doctor told me that if I kept playing, I'd be finished, but to a kid who grew up on a farm in east Texas, I felt as if the Super Bowl was my only chance to really make it big. Besides, the second-string quarterback was younger and had two good legs, and every time I was away, it was a little harder to come back, a little harder to re-establish my position as quarterback.''

Jamie saw the wry twist of his lips. "So they pumped me full of painkillers, and I played. We won. Afterward, I had that third surgery, and they informed me that my football days were over.''

"So you're saying in a roundabout way that if you're away from your business like you were from the game, someone will come in and take away the place you've made for yourself.''

"Exactly.''

"At this point, I doubt that, Mr. Bishop. After all, you own the entire operation. And it seems to me that not taking care of your knee resulted in terrible waste.''

"It was my choice to make,'' he told her with an edge to his voice.

She nodded. "And you make the choices for Chris.''

"Correct.''

"But are your choices the right ones? Look, Mr. Bishop, your name is synonymous with football in one way or the other. It's your tie to the past and your future. A secure future. Can't you give the same chance to Chris?''

"By sending him back to public school?''

"Yes.''

"The public school system isn't always the answer.''

"What do you mean?" she asked, her brows drawing together in a frown.

Mitch looked into her questioning eyes. It was hard to imagine any man denying her anything, but he had no intention of spilling his guts to a virtual stranger. He took a healthy swallow of his drink and leveled her with a steady gaze, trying to decide how to answer.

"Ah," she said on a slightly sarcastic note, "I think I detect a hint of that malady so often seen in the rich and famous."

"And what's that, Ms. Carr?"

"Public school snobbery."

Mitch's first inclination was to let her think what she would, but something wouldn't let him go that far. He liked her. Really liked her determination and fire. He'd enjoyed this round of fighting with her.

He smiled. "I'll tell you what, Ms. Carr, just to prove you're wrong, I'll compromise. I'll let Chris come back to school until there's an opening at Barstow."

Jamie blinked in surprise, unable to understand what had brought about the sudden change in him. Still, his limited concession was better than nothing, and maybe, given time, she could change his mind. Had she misjudged him, then? A slight smile that held both disappointment and a trace of victory curved her lips. She held out her hand. Mitch's closed around it. His hand was warm and callused, and his grip was firm.

"I'll take the compromise, Mr. Bishop, and in the meantime, we'll set up an appointment so you can see just what we hope Chris will accomplish this year."

"You won't change my mind, Ms. Carr."

This time her smile was filled with challenge. "We'll see, Mr. Bishop. We'll see."

For a long time after Jamie left, Mitch sat in his chair before the fire, nursing another glass of whiskey and staring into the flames. If he'd been troubled before her arrival, it was nothing compared to the chaos of his thoughts now.

"Can't you delegate . . . ?"

He shook his head. How could she possibly know how important his company was? He'd been alone except for Joyce after their mother died when he was eleven. And then, when Joyce had married four years later, he'd been alone again in spite of the fact that she and Michael both still cared for him. Football had become his life, and when that had come to an end, he hadn't known what to do with himself. It was only when the owner of the team, grateful to Mitch for leading them to the top after nine years of obscurity, had come to him in the hospital and offered to lend him money to buy into a business that Mitch had felt there might be something in the world for him after all.

Although he'd hated to borrow, he had taken the offer and bought a failing sporting goods manufacturing company in Chicago. The same willpower and determination that had seen him through the final game had enabled him to make a success of the business. And now, eleven years later, he had not only the Chicago plant but also a newer one in Baton Rouge.

But he couldn't expect Jamie Carr to understand. She fairly oozed confidence and determination. She

looked like someone it wouldn't be pleasant to tangle
with . . . unless it was in bed.

The errant thought, slipping so easily into his mind,
surprised Mitch. He recalled the way her tongue had
slicked over her lips in unconscious invitation, the way
the wind had blown the hair across that moistness, and
the way he admitted now—but had refused to then—
that he'd wanted to push it away from her face and
cover her mouth with his. He swore softly. He couldn't
remember having such an immediate and startling response to a woman in years. Why?

Was it the way she tossed her curls and brushed
them away from her ivory complexion? Or—ever one
to love a challenge himself—was it the flashing lights
of defiance and will that lured him? Maybe he was
drawn to her because she was so different from the
women he usually dated, women who were career ori-
ented, on their way up, determined to climb to the top
of the corporate ladder no matter what the cost.

Mitch stretched his bad leg out toward the fire. They
had their purpose, those women. Just like any woman,
they were warm in bed. And if their bodies were the
only things they were willing to give and his was all
they wanted in return, so much the better. He wasn't
looking for a business competitor—or a wife. He'd
had more than his share of loving and leaving—from
both sides of the fence.

He had what he wanted. Financial success. A place
in the world. A world that wouldn't dare laugh at him
as it had during the years before he'd been diagnosed
as dyslexic, before he'd discovered he didn't have to be
able to read to throw a football.

No, his life was exactly the way he wanted it: without emotional complications. He didn't want anyone in his life who would dig too deeply into his well-hidden emotional reserves, which was another reason having Chris around bothered him so. The boy was already a threat to his self-imposed emotional exile. Chris could breach his carefully erected defenses with a single smile.

His thoughts returned to Jamie Carr and the smile that had changed her from a stern, defensive woman to a woman who looked an impish eighteen.

Mitch rose and refilled his glass, hoping the liquor would dull the ache in his leg and put Jamie Carr and his instant attraction to her into perspective. He got his wish some two drinks later, just as the clock struck eleven.

She was merely another pretty woman; he was a healthy, normal male. There wasn't anything wrong with wanting to check out the promise of slender hips and rounded breasts that her sweater hid. There was nothing the matter with wanting to see if her lips tasted as ripe and sweet as they looked, and if the fire in her eyes could be kindled by the touch of his hands. The fact that he did want to check her out was surprising in itself, considering no woman had stirred his hormones in a long time.

Actually, he'd begun to wonder if something was the matter with him. It had been months since he'd spent the night with a woman, and even longer since he'd met one who really interested him. He'd begun to wonder if he was working too hard or if there was something physically wrong with him. But now, thanks to his instant response to Chris's pretty teacher, he knew his fears were unfounded.

Still, he had to keep his realization in perspective. Just because he had responded to her didn't mean there was anything more to it than a physical attraction, and he'd best not forget it. It had nothing to do with the way she'd been with Chris. Nothing to do with the way her eyes flashed with challenge, or the way her unique scent reminded him of all the good, sweet things in life. Sexual attraction was the only pull he felt for her. The only one.

Jamie closed her eyes and sank back against the pillows. Mitchell Bishop's face floated tantalizingly against the screen of her mind. She couldn't recall when she'd seen bone structure so superbly masculine. Thick, dark eyebrows rode above a straight nose and well-defined nostrils. He had sculpted cheekbones and a square jaw, and his chin, dimpled à la Kirk Douglas, sat below a mouth that was Sean Connery sexy.

The moment she'd set eyes on him, her inner warning system had gone off with blaring sirens, clanging bells and flashing lights that all signaled danger. Shocked by the intensity of her reaction to him, she'd licked suddenly dry lips and instinctively taken a step backward. It had taken every morsel of willpower she possessed to keep from falling under the spell cast by the come-hither warmth glowing in his eyes.

Still, once she'd regained possession of her temporarily lost sanity, she'd presented her case for Chris very well. Mitchell Bishop hadn't managed to get past her guard again, even though his attitude made it obvious that he was a hard case. If Chris hadn't come in and said what he had, she might never have convinced his uncle that keeping him in public school was the best thing, at least for now. She smiled at the memory of Chris's happy face when he'd first seen her. That was the sort of thing that made her job worthwhile, the sort of thing that filled her empty life and made it worth living.

Without warning, another smile flashed through her mind, momentarily nudging aside her concern for Chris. Mitch's devastating smile as he'd stood in the doorway. There was no denying he was handsome. Charismatic. Worldly. And as hard as the finely chiseled shape of his mouth.

"Hi, honey. What can I do for you?"

The memory of his casual question brought back the anger that had suffused her when he spoke it. Staring through the darkness at the star-spangled ceiling, Jamie fumed. *Honey.* She'd be willing to bet a year's salary he called every female under eighty honey. Mitch Bishop was the kind of man she'd declared taboo five years ago.

So why did your heart skip a beat when he looked at you? Her inner self demanded an answer.

Just because I have no intention of getting involved with a man like that again doesn't mean I can't react, does it? My hormones are packed away, not dead.

She took a deep breath and imagined she got a whiff of exotic, masculine cologne. Disgusted, she punched her pillow and turned onto her stomach. Much later, she fell asleep.

Her dreams were filled with Mitchell Bishop.

And to her surprise and pleasure, his lips weren't so hard after all.

Chapter Three

Jamie licked her lips, trying her best to ignore the churning in her stomach and concentrate on the information before her. Without thinking, she reached for a lock of hair and began to wind it around her finger. Mitchell Bishop would be here any minute, and she knew without a doubt that if she hoped to convince him to let Chris stay in public school, she had to be better than just adequately prepared. It would take more than words on paper to change his mind about sending Chris to Barstow.

She glanced around the room. The twelve children were working quietly for a change, diligently reproducing the letter S on lined paper. Resting her forehead in her palm, Jamie forced her attention back to the pages of Chris's file.

A knock at the door sent her gaze and that of a now disrupted class toward the sound, and before she could reply Mitchell Bishop stepped into the room.

His brown eyes unerringly slammed into her green ones. Her twisting finger stilled in her hair. The rehearsed answers to the questions she thought he might ask fled her mind. Her breathing faltered. She'd forgotten how warm and compelling his eyes were. Forgotten the breadth of his shoulders. Forgotten...

"Mitz!"

Chris's voice brought Jamie from her trance. Mitch's gaze flew toward his nephew, whose happiness at seeing his uncle was apparent from the smile on his face. His arms spread, he got up from his seat and started for Mitch. Under the circumstances, Jamie didn't have the heart to tell him to sit back down.

Mitch flicked her a questioning look and, seeing her soft expression, knelt. He took Chris into his arms, gave him a brief squeeze and ruffled his hair. "How's it goin', tiger?"

"Awwight."

"That's great!" With one hand still on Chris's shoulder, he stood. "Am I too early?"

Sparing a glance at the clock, Jamie shook her head. "Not really."

"Go home?" Chris asked expectantly.

"Not now, Chris," Jamie said. "Your uncle and I are going to have a meeting."

Chris's mouth sloped down. "Aw..."

Jamie turned to a woman seated across the room. "Will you come here, Marie?"

The young woman, who looked to be in her twenties, rose and came toward Jamie. Mitch realized with something of a start that she, too, was retarded to some extent.

"Mr. Bishop, this is my aide, Marie Cathcart. Marie, this is Chris Decker's uncle, Mr. Bishop."

"Hello, Marie," Mitch said. Her response was shy, barely audible.

"Mr. Bishop and I are going to Miss Huckabee's room for a conference. Will you see that the children stay seated and finish their papers?" The woman nodded, and Jamie continued, "If they finish, there are some drawings on my desk they can color. All right?"

"Yes, Ms. Carr," Marie replied.

Jamie smiled. "Good. Chris, go on back to your seat. Uncle Mitch will be back in a little while."

For a moment she thought he might show them his stubborn streak, but with another dejected "Aw" he turned and did as she asked.

Jamie rose and picked up a folder. And almost knocked over a bud vase. She righted it with an unsteady hand and glanced at Mitch from the corner of her eye. Would he interpret her clumsiness as nervousness and assume she was worried over the outcome of the meeting?

If so, he didn't show it. He stood there, dressed in tan slacks and a forest-green striped shirt topped with a brown tweed sports coat, which was pushed out of the way for the hands residing with casual negligence in the pockets of his pants, the personification of male confidence.

Jamie's tongue slid over her dry lips, and she tried to calm the increased cadence of her heartbeats. She wouldn't think about how his expensive slacks pulled so tautly over the evidence of his sex or the way she found herself longing to see if her fingertip fit the dimple in his chin. Instead, she straightened, turned and asked with false brightness and determination, "Ready?"

Mitch responded with a single unsmiling nod, fighting the growing attraction conceived in his doorway more than a week before. Jamie looked trendy and exceedingly pretty in suede boots, a long, western-style chambray skirt and matching shirt decorated with silver studs at the yoke.

Rounding the desk and being very careful not to look into his eyes, she moved toward him, her stylish faux silver and turquoise belt jingling as she walked.

A curious vulnerability invaded her once she stepped from behind the barricade of her desk. A vulnerability that quickened as Mitch matched her stride for silent stride down the hall and through the doorway leading to the borrowed classroom.

Once inside, Jamie reached out to move a stray chair nearer the desk, but before she could, Mitch was beside her, grasping the chair back, his hand accidentally brushing hers in the process. A jolt of electricity shot up her arm and sent her gaze winging to his. Her disbelief in such elemental chemistry was forever smashed to smithereens.

His brown eyes smiled. "Got it."

Her hands dropped. "Thanks," she said, going to the desk and sitting down. She opened the folder with a deliberate no-nonsense attitude while Mitch seated himself across from her.

Jamie pushed the folder toward him. "This is Chris's IEP—Individualized Education Program—

that we worked out at the beginning of the school year, based on what he accomplished last year,'' she explained, turning it sideways so he could see as she pointed things out.

"That looks a little awkward." The words were barely out of his mouth before he was carrying his chair around the desk and positioning it beside hers. Close beside hers.

She turned her shoulders slightly away from him and did her best to ignore the alluring scent of the cologne she remembered so well. Clearing her throat, she pointed to the bottom right-hand corner of the first page.

Mitch's gaze followed, and his throat tightened at the sight of Joyce and Michael's signatures.

"This basically explains Chris's long-term goal for school. Signing this means that your sister and her husband realized Chris would never be able to pass the state's minimum basic skills tests."

"What's that?"

"Students in the regular school program are tested periodically to see if they've learned the basics and to see if they can be passed on to the next grade," Jamie explained. "Because Chris is mildly retarded, he can't work on grade level. He needs one-on-one instruction and an adapted curriculum, although he is with regular classes for PE, lunch, assemblies and recess."

"What's an adapted curriculum?"

She glanced at him and pushed her hair away from her face, exposing the delicate curve of her neck, which bore a tiny brown mole, and a small ear bearing a dangly silver and turquoise earring.

"We'll get to that in a moment. I just want you to be certain that you understand our long-term goal."

"Which is?" he asked, dragging his attention from her throat to look directly into her eyes.

"Chris will never be able to get a high school diploma, Mr. Bishop. What he will be striving for is a Certificate of Achievement."

Mitch nodded, but she could see the doubt and questions in his eyes.

"Chris is in an adapted physical education program two days a week, where they work on both his gross and fine motor skills. The rest of the week he's in with a regular second-grade class. He also sees a speech therapist twice a week. You'll meet those teachers later."

He nodded again.

"If you understand and just sign these, we'll move on," Jamie said, pushing the paper closer and offering him a ballpoint pen.

"Why do I have to sign?"

She turned to look at him. "Because you're Chris's guardian now."

"But he's only going to be here until there's an opening in Barstow."

As if she'd forgotten.

"I understand that, Mr. Bishop," she said in a cool tone—something of a miracle really, since she was doing a slow boil at the mention of Barstow. "But rules are rules. Please." She held out the pen again.

Mitch looked into her stormy eyes and felt another ripple of admiration. She was a professional to her toes, despite the fact that she sometimes looked like a high school student instead of a teacher. He took the pen, holding her gaze for long seconds before he signed his name with a bold, decisive scrawl below his sister's.

"Thank you." Jamie put the page on the bottom of the stack and rolled the chair back so she could face him better.

"Basically," she began, "even though Chris is eight, at the start of the school year he was at 1.0 grade level, or the beginning of first grade. He was a nonreader but knew some letters and sounds by sight from last year, probably because your sister worked with him. He is reading a few words by sight now, and by the way," she tossed out with a challenging look, "you should be letting him read to you at night. By the end of the year we hope to have him up to a 1.3 level."

"I'm not certain I understand," Mitch said.

"First grade, third month."

"First grade, third month!" he exploded, vaulting from the seat and glaring down at her. "He's eight years old, dammit! What kind of teaching is that, anyway?"

Jamie was beginning to realize that Mitchell Bishop had little idea of what caring for Chris really involved. "Very good teaching, Mr. Bishop," she said calmly. "Surely you're familiar enough with Chris's background to realize he won't ever progress beyond the intellectual level of about six years old."

Shock hit Mitch squarely between the eyes. He'd heard Joyce talk about Chris's condition, but he hadn't paid careful attention to it, because he'd never known he would be directly involved. Shame followed closely on the heels of the shock and was quickly overcome by a sudden irrational anger. He was mad at fate, or God, or whatever had made Chris the way he was. Angry at Joyce for dying. And at himself for not knowing how to handle this new turn of events. And he was furious with Jamie Carr for making him feel this sense of inadequacy.

With anger in full rein, he sat back down and leaned toward Jamie, belligerence in the set of his broad shoulders. "If that's the case, and he needs one-on-one attention, it seems as if Barstow would be the best place for him. Don't you agree, Ms. Carr?"

His voice was silky smooth and deceivingly soft, but Jamie heard the thread of steel woven through it. Refusing to flinch from either his anger or his unrelenting gaze, she replied, "The best place for Chris is where he'll get what he needs to develop to his full potential. Don't you agree?"

The answer knocked Mitch off-balance. He'd expected her to defend the public school system again.

Before he could recover, she asked, "Is there someone at Barstow to sit with Chris in front of the fire and let him read to him or her?"

Once again Mitch stifled his surprise. Was there? He didn't know, but he damn sure wasn't going to let her know that, just as he wasn't going to let her know how badly her questions were shaking his beliefs.

"I'm sure that whatever their reading program is, it's thorough and effective or they wouldn't be in business. Actually, Ms. Carr, if the waiting list is any indication of quality, it's an excellent school," he told her. The look on his face was one the other team had always known meant trouble during his football days.

"I've never implied otherwise."

He rose and plunged his hands into the pockets of his slacks, his height and breadth guaranteeing intimidation. "Wrong. You've never *said* otherwise. You've implied plenty."

Jamie straightened in her chair and looked up at him, her green eyes smoky with the beginnings of her own brand of anger. "Are you saying that—"

"Mostly," he said, cutting through her protests, "you've implied that Chris would be better off here than in a school geared for and totally devoted to educating children like—"

Trembling, Jamie leaped to her feet, slicing through his speech with her own defense. "I can assure you, Mr. Bishop, that I'm totally devoted to educating—"

"—him," Mitch finished as if she'd never spoken. "It's a perfect environment for Chris."

She crossed her arms across her breasts in an effort to still her shaking. "It isn't a perfect environment for him. Not at this stage in his life."

Watching the color rise in her cheeks and the sparks fly in her eyes as her anger built, Mitch felt that insane, irrational desire stirring inside him once more. It was ludicrous...ridiculous...and destined for nowhere. He had the hots for Chris's teacher. He began to laugh, laughter directed at himself.

He was laughing! Jamie realized in amazement. Butting heads with Mitchell Bishop was tough. After all, he was used to it. Jamie felt like throwing up her hands in defeat. Instead she sighed and tried to convince him one last time.

"There's a whole world out there, Mr. Bishop, and whether you like it or not, Chris has to live and function in it at some point in his life."

Something about her tugged at the heartstrings he'd knotted years before. It made him too aware that, beneath the veneer of toughness he showed the world, he was a soft touch. "I understand that."

"Then prepare him for it."

"That's what I'm trying to do."

"Then keep him mainstreamed, not shut up in a sterile atmosphere where he won't be challenged by the world around him."

"Challenged?"

"Yes. He needs to interact with the world. He needs to learn to make his own way."

A picture of Jamie's helper, Marie Cathcart, flashed through Mitch's mind. Was she making her way? How had she come this far? How responsible was she? And could Chris ever hope to be left in charge of anything? The magnitude of the changes in his life that Chris's presence demanded stretched out before Mitch. Overwhelmed him. It was his turn to sigh, his turn to feel defeat. He sat back down. He hadn't intended to give one inch, just as he hadn't intended to let Chris come back to public school. Nevertheless he heard himself say, "I think we both want what's best for Chris. Now we have to establish just what that is."

Puzzled by his abrupt about-face, Jamie eased into her chair and waited to see what curve he would throw her next.

"Well?" he said at last.

"Well, what?"

"Let's hear it. You said you'd explain Chris's adapted curriculum. As I told you before, you have until there's an opening in Barstow to convince me that leaving Chris here is the best thing for him."

* * *

So she's pretty, intelligent, dedicated and has a temper that makes you wonder what other fires she has hidden inside. There are a hundred other women in Baton Rouge just like her.

Cursing under his breath, Mitch tried to gather his thoughts so he could concentrate on the stack of work that needed his immediate attention. Impossible. He'd worked harder and accomplished less the last two-plus weeks than he could ever remember... all because he couldn't get Jamie Carr out of his mind.

She intrigued him in a way no woman had in years. He was interested in getting to know her better. Definitely interested. And Chris had nothing to do with it. He was fascinated by the flash of green fire in her eyes when she was angry; he admired the way she stood by her convictions. He could relate to her dedication. Dedication was the ingredient it took to be a success at whatever you chose to do; he admired it in a man or a woman.

"So what's your problem?"

Mitch looked up and saw Ian Forrest, his cousin Karen's husband, standing in the doorway. What the devil was Ian doing at the offices of Bishop's, and how in hell had he gotten past the receptionist unannounced? No doubt that smooth British charm of his, and the easy endearments that tripped off his golden tongue. Mitch urged a smile he was far from feeling to his lips. "Hey! Come on in."

Ian moved across the room with the inbred grace passed down through generations of blue British blood and seated himself across from Mitch. Then he pulled a thin cigar from his inside jacket pocket, fixed Mitch with a determined look and asked, "Well?"

"Well, what?"

"What's your problem?"

One corner of Mitch's mouth hiked up in a lop-sided smile. "What makes you think I have a problem?"

"You haven't called, haven't been around in God only knows how long. As a matter of fact, Karen said she's hardly heard a word from you since—" he paused momentarily at the bleakness that passed like a dark cloud over Mitch's features "—the funeral."

"I've been busy."

Ian placed the cigar between his finely shaped lips. His lighter flared briefly, and he inhaled a draught of smoke. There was a considering light in his blue eyes as he exhaled it slowly. "Karen was afraid something was wrong."

"Why would anything be wrong?" Mitch asked dryly. "Just because I'm suddenly the parent of an eight-year-old retarded child, why would anything be wrong?"

"Sarcasm doesn't become you, my friend," Ian told him. "Honesty is far more your style."

"Honesty, huh?" Mitch said with a bitter laugh. His voice lost its cynicism, but it was in his eyes as surely as it was in his heart. "Then how about this? I'm in over my head, Ian. I don't know how to relate to Chris. I'm ignorant, he's stubborn, and—"

Ian's smile was wry. "That'll do for starters," he said, interrupting Mitch's list. There was compassion and honesty in his own eyes as he demanded, "Why the bloody hell haven't you called and asked us to help?"

Mitch's fingers plowed through his hair. "I've been...coping."

"Not very well by the sounds of things."

"It'll get better. I'm sending him to Barstow as soon as there's an opening. That'll solve a lot of problems."

Ian was thoughtfully quiet for a moment.

"What's the matter?" Mitch quizzed.

Ian shrugged. "I don't know. I suspect I was wondering how Barstow would help Chris."

"What do you mean?" Mitch asked, uncertain he really wanted to hear what his friend had to say.

"Are you quite sure it would be best for Chris to send him away right now?"

Another round of bitter laughter echoed through the room. "You sound like Jamie Carr."

Ian didn't miss the hint of anger in Mitch's eyes. "Who's Jamie Carr?"

"Chris's teacher at public school."

"Ah. I gather she isn't thrilled over the prospect of Chris's being sent to a boarding school, either."

Mitch leaned back in his leather chair and folded his arms across his broad chest. "Yeah. You could say that."

"It's something you should give considerable thought," Ian said.

Mitch had always respected Ian's opinion, but the fact that he seemed to be siding with Jamie didn't sit well. "Did anyone ever tell you you can be a royal pain in the—"

"Many times," the Englishman said with an unruffled smile. He tapped his cigar over a large crystal ashtray. "So tell me about Chris's teacher. She must be a good one if she was concerned enough to come to you about Chris."

"She is." That much he could honestly say. "She's also dedicated, stubborn and argumentative."

"She'd have to be to talk you into something you were against. How old is this dragon, anyway?"

"That's the kicker," Mitch said with a weary smile. "She isn't a dragon. She's probably in her late twenties and looks eighteen."

"Ah. Pretty, I gather?" Ian said, nodding as he did so.

"Passably," Mitch grumbled, knowing she was much more than passably pretty, as the tightening in his loins reminded him every time he came near her.

"Short?" Ian knew Mitch's preference for petite women.

"Tall." As if he were measuring how tall she was compared to him, he held his hand horizontally just below his nose. "About here."

Ian's fair eyebrows rose. "Blond and curvy?"

"Almost-black, curly hair . . . and small busted."

"Ah. The lure of the unfamiliar."

"And what does that cryptic statement mean?"

"Nothing at all," Ian responded with feigned innocence.

"Look," Mitch began, "if you think I'm interested in her, you're wrong."

"Of course."

"I mean it. She isn't my type at all. Besides not being petite, blond and beautiful, she's too hottempered and mouthy for my liking."

"Methinks you doth protest too much," Ian misquoted, tongue in cheek.

"Is that right?" Mitch asked. "Well, methinks you're too damn nosy."

Ian mimed a fencing thrust. "Touché."

The laughter was gone from Mitch's eyes as he urged, "Ease up, man."

Ian was smart enough to know when to stop. He held up his hands, palms outward. "Consider me eased."

In spite of his irritation, Mitch found himself laughing at Ian's phraseology. It was impossible to stay mad at him. He was genuinely likable, and his sense of humor and the protective way he'd helped Karen overcome the scars from a drunken and abusive father covered a multitude of sins in Mitch's book.

"So," Ian said, rising and stubbing out the cigar, "now that we've established that, I'm to tell Karen you've been up to your shoulder pads in work and that you'll be to dinner on Wednesday evening, right?"

Knowing an evening spent at the Forrests' was the only way back into Karen's good graces, Mitch nodded. "Right."

"And," Ian tacked on, apparently unable to drop the subject entirely, "will you be bringing anyone?"

Mitch thought of Jamie and how much he'd like to try to get her eyes to light up for him the way they did for Chris. It had been a long time since he'd had to pursue a woman. He hadn't liked the feeling at twenty; he liked it even less now.

"No." His voice was firm, final. "I won't be bringing anyone."

* * *

Ian had been gone for more than three hours, yet his question of whether or not Mitch would be bringing anyone to dinner still played through Mitch's mind. Why shouldn't he call Jamie and ask her to go to Ian and Karen's with him? he wondered, forcing himself to look at the situation with some of the honesty Ian had demanded. She *was* the first woman he'd found interesting in a long time. Besides, it wouldn't hurt him to apologize for losing his temper during their meeting.

He shoved back his cuff and checked the time. Four-thirty. She should be home from school by now. He looked up her number, punched it into the phone and listened to it ring. Three times. His fingers drummed against the polished surface of the desk. Four. He stared at the ceiling. He took a deep breath, exhaled it slowly on the sixth ring and was about to hang up when he heard the receiver being lifted from its cradle.

"Hello?"

She sounded breathless, he thought. Breathless and . . . undeniably sexy.

"Hello, Jamie. It's Mitch Bishop."

The silence coming through the lines when he gave his name was almost tangible. He wanted to ask if she'd been running, if she'd just gotten home. He wanted to ask her how her day had been and if she had been as unable to forget him as he had her. His thoughts appalled him, unnerved him. And of course, he didn't.

"Are you busy?"

Jamie blotted the perspiration from her face with the towel hanging around her neck. "Not really. I was doing my aerobics."

"I won't keep you long, then. I just wanted to call and apologize for losing my temper the other day," he said. It was a poor excuse, since he'd stayed another twenty minutes while she explained more about Chris's routine at school. "After all, you were just presenting the facts as you see them."

"It's all right. I hope I helped," she said, recognizing the ruse for what it was and wondering why he'd really called.

He laughed softly. "Did anyone ever tell you that you could pass for a high school student?"

"Often." Her voice held irritation.

"Oops! Sorry. I didn't know looking young was irritating."

"Well, it is. Extremely."

"Hmm," Mitch said. "What about looking pretty? Is that irritating, too?"

"No. Not if whoever thinks so is sincere."

"Are you saying you don't think my compliments are sincere?"

Her tone matched his, brittle lightness for brittle lightness, yet each was trying to impress the other. Mitch with his genuine sincerity. Jamie with her determination not to be taken in by what she considered his casual charm.

"Unlike the hordes of women in your life, Mr. Bishop, I'm not easily manipulated with pretty words."

"And in spite of what you think, I do not have a different woman every night. By the way," he tacked on, "do you think you could call me Mitch?"

"I'd rather not call you at all," she said with feigned sweetness.

His voice was like spilled cream on satin as he said, "Then I'll have to change your mind, won't I?"

"You can try. But let me warn you, I'm not the kind of woman you're used to."

Mitch laughed softly. He was loving every minute of their verbal sparring. "How do you know what kind of woman I'm used to?"

"Why, *Mitch*, you must know that in some ways Baton Rouge is a small town. News about local celebrities always travels far and wide."

He chuckled again. "You're right. I am used to a different kind of woman, but that doesn't mean you're any less...interesting."

"Me, a schoolteacher, interesting?" she repeated, laughing briefly.

Mitch thought about that for a moment. Somehow the conversation had lost its baiting, teasing quality and had become personal, serious. "You say that as if you don't think you are."

"It isn't that I don't think I am. I know I'm not," she corrected. "I'm not interesting. Not beautiful. Not sexy."

"According to whom?" he asked, not believing what he was hearing. Personally, he thought she was as sexy as they came, especially when she was riled. He thought about telling her so, but decided that would be jumping the gun.

"My former husband, for one," she said honestly.

"You've been married?" That was something he'd never considered.

"Few people get to be my age without trying it at least once," she told him smoothly, ignoring the pain the memory of her failure always brought. "What about you?"

"No. Never. I only came close once." He winced slightly at the memory of his last foray into trust and emotional vulnerability.

"Having too good a time with all those beautiful, together women?" she pressed, struggling to regain the tempo of the earlier part of their conversation.

"No," he countered. "Trying to keep out of the clutches of those beautiful, together women."

Jamie's laughter was disbelieving.

"Why do I get the idea you don't have a very high opinion of me?" he asked, simultaneously wondering why the hell her opinion of him should matter.

Jamie realized she'd overstepped the bounds of politeness their short association allowed. His women— type or lack of—were none of her business. "I'm sorry. I don't know you well enough to have an opinion of you, and I certainly don't know you well enough to question your love life."

"That can be remedied."

Jamie's heart skipped a beat and then started pounding at the inference of his statement and the sound of his bedroom voice. Her own voice was barely audible as she asked, "What do you mean?"

"I called to tell you I was sorry and ask if you'd like to go to my cousin's for dinner Wednesday evening. She and her husband invited me to bring a guest."

She didn't speak for so long that Mitch asked, "Jamie? Are you still there?"

"Y-yes."

"Well, would you like to go?"

She wanted to say yes, desperately wanted to, but the bitter memory of her past romantic failures hung over her like a pall.

"I'm sorry," she said at last. "I make it a rule to never date a student's parent."

"I'm not a parent."

"That's splitting hairs."

"Chris will be going," he tossed in, hoping that having Chris as a buffer would tilt the scales in his favor.

"Chris will be going." The casually offered statement halted her mental seesaw. Disappointment, sharp and pungent, pierced her. It was all beginning to make sense.

Mitch was going to his cousin's. If she and her husband were in Mitch's social strata, they probably had Sevres vases and Lalique crystal on every table. More than likely Mitch hadn't taken Chris there before and wasn't sure how the child would react or if he could handle him. Enter Jamie Carr, fool extraordinaire, always willing to take on ready-made families in the blink of an eye for the love of a handsome man. Hadn't she done it twice already? It was bad enough that she'd married debonair Chad and had come to love his daughter Lisa as her own, only to lose the girl once Jamie had outlived her usefulness in Chad's life. But then she'd nearly walked into the same deadly trap again with Paul, a handsome widower who'd almost but not quite convinced Jamie he wanted a wife as much as he'd needed a full-time mother for his two adorable children.

Common sense told her Mitch couldn't have known about her past, but her intellect told her he was smart enough to see how good she was with kids, and he certainly knew how much she cared about them. He might not consciously realize he was looking for help, but she was conscious of it, and that was enough.

"I'm sorry. I can't."

"Won't."

She closed her eyes against the controlled anger she heard in his voice. "All right, won't. As I said, I don't see students' single fathers socially."

"And you never break the rules?"

"Not if I can help it."

Mitch forced a casual laugh he was far from feeling. "Okay then, Teach, I'll let you go, but I want you to know I'm persistent. Maybe I'll catch you one day when your defenses are low."

Ignoring his statement, she said, "We'll be testing again soon. I'll let you know how Chris does when we finish."

"Fine."

Goodbyes were said, and receivers were cradled simultaneously. Mitch swore softly and violently. Jamie sat staring at the telephone for long moments.

She'd done the right thing, hadn't she? She was a smart twenty-eight now, not a vulnerable twenty-three. Some things were simply poison to some people, and socially and financially well-off men were poison to her. They always had been, and she had no reason to think things would be any different with Mitch Bishop. Besides, he had another strike against him. Chris. As much as she loved the child, she wouldn't let herself be used again.

The next man she got involved with would love her for herself, not for her ability to cope with his kids. It was a promise she'd made to herself years ago, and she vowed she wouldn't break it . . . no matter how badly she wanted to.

Chapter Four

February typified south Louisiana winter at its finest. Some days still held a definite nip, but all over Baton Rouge crocuses peeked through the ground in sun-warmed places, and tender shoots of green grass poked delicate necks through the rain-softened earth.

On a Wednesday, one week after she might have gone with Mitch to his cousin's for dinner, Jamie sat at her desk watching a robin—definitely a Weight Watchers candidate—hopping over the ground in search of a foolhardy insect. Chilly or not, spring was in the air, and the anticipation of renewal brought an inevitable surge of happiness.

Or, Jamie asked herself with a bit of smugness, was the happiness she felt the result of the testing she had just finished and the fact that her students had done so well? It was probably both, but she couldn't help wanting to gloat, especially over two students' progress. Carrie Hamilton and Chris Decker had gone beyond her hopes. With three and a half months of the school year left to go, they had already reached most of the goals Jamie and the other teachers who worked with them had set.

Her soft laughter crowded the quiet from the room, empty now of children who, along with a congratulatory gift and a progress report, had been sent home for the day.

Her glowing eyes scanned Chris's reports again with something close to disbelief. His speech teacher had hoped his communications skills—using *the* in sentences, adding the proper endings to words and using the possessive and past tense—would improve by eighty percent, and they had.

His physical education teacher was pleased that his motor skills had improved so that he was able to hit an overhead target four out of five times on five separate occasions. He could also hop on one foot the designated time and usually catch both large and small balls. The PE teacher had also found out that Chris loved to race the other children and had suggested that he train for the upcoming Special Olympics.

Observation, her own testing and the Brigance test proved that in Jamie's classes Chris's improvement was even more impressive. His understanding of greater and less, the recognition of money and his ability to associate zero to ten with their corresponding numerals had slightly exceeded her goal of eighty percent accuracy. The basic concepts of wet and dry, over and under and many others had been a breeze for Chris. He could auditorily associate seventeen letters of the alphabet with their sounds—seven more than she had hoped for.

But the thing she was the most proud of was his reading. She'd hoped he could visually and orally recognize twenty words from the Dolch list of common words with eighty percent accuracy, but Chris had surprised her by being correct closer to ninety percent of the time.

She read the results for the dozenth time, a wide grin on her face. All in all, she was pleased with what she'd helped her class achieve. No. She was more than pleased. She was ecstatic.

Put that in your pipe and smoke it, Mr. High and Mighty Bishop. She laughed again and slapped Chris's folder shut.

"I knew it would come to this one day," Leah said from behind her.

Jamie turned toward her friend, her face reflecting her happiness. "Come to what?"

"Obviously, you've flipped."

"Why?"

Leah, who was on her way home, entered the room carrying a diet cola and a briefcase. Easing into one of the student desks, she set down her drink and raised her eyebrows. "You were sitting in an empty room, laughing. Pretty strange, wouldn't you say?"

Jamie's smile widened. "Not if you knew what I was laughing about."

"I see. And do you plan on telling me what's so funny, or do I have to play a guessing game?"

"I've just sent home progress reports."

Leah nodded and extracted a Twinkie from her case. "Well, I certainly agree that's a relief—but laughing?"

"My kids did great. Better than great. They did fantastic!" She leaned back in her chair, crossed her arms across her breasts and propped her feet on her desk in a cocky manner. "I'm a good special ed teacher. No, a great special ed teacher."

"Imagine," Leah said, licking a blob of creamy filling from her bottom lip, "a great teacher and modest, too."

"I know," Jamie said, with humor dancing in her eyes. "Simply amazing, isn't it?" She and Leah broke into giggles, which quickly escalated into end-of-the-day giddiness.

"Stop!" Leah dabbed at the corners of her eyes. "I have to go shopping, and I don't want to look like a wreck."

Jamie sobered and wiped her own eyes. "I guess laughter's as good a way as any to release pressure."

"Pressure? What kind of pressure? Sam thinks you're the greatest thing since bubble gum, and I know he pretty much leaves you and your methods alone."

Jamie nodded. "Yeah. He does. The pressure isn't coming from Sam. It's self-induced."

Leah crumpled the cake wrapper and tossed it toward the wastebasket. "I know you demand a lot from yourself, but what, exactly, do you mean?"

"Mitch Bishop."

"Mitch Bishop?" Leah repeated. "What about him? I thought everything was hunky-dory since you got him to let Chris come back."

A slight smile curved Jamie's lips. "I wouldn't say things were hunky-anything. As a matter of fact, things are pretty sticky."

"What do you mean?"

"Surely Sam told you that Chris is back only temporarily. His uncle is bound and determined to put the child in Barstow, but he did say I could try to persuade him to leave Chris here."

"And your test results are obviously good and should sway him," Leah said.

"*Should* being the operative word."

"Right. So how are things sticky?"

Jamie looked at Leah. "He asked me out."

"Mitch Bishop asked you out, and you didn't tell me?" Leah squealed, jumping up from the small desk so quickly that she almost knocked it over.

"I'd never go," Jamie assured her quickly. "It isn't good to get involved with parents. Besides, all we'd do is argue over which is best, private school or public."

"Forget school. Go. Concentrate on the man," Leah said, her eyes gleaming.

"If he weren't Chris's uncle, I just might consider it," Jamie conceded. "He's handsome, has a sense of humor, and seems pretty nice—when he isn't mad," she qualified.

Leah advanced toward Jamie with feigned anger. "*Nice* is not a word you use in connection with a man like Mitch Bishop. Now, tell me everything!"

Jamie sighed. "Actually, there's nothing to tell. He wanted me to go to his cousin's for dinner."

"You should have gone."

"He was taking Chris."

"So? That would've been fine. It's hard for a man to make a pass with a kid in tow."

Jamie decided to put all her cards on the table. "I figured he wanted me to go along as a built-in baby-sitter."

Leah's surprise was evident. "Jamie, that isn't fair."

"I know. But I can't afford any more mistakes."

Leah nodded. "I understand being careful, but there's a limit to anything. You're going to have to break down at some point and give a guy a chance."

"Maybe so, but not this time. Not with Mitch Bishop." Her tone held no compromise. "I made myself a promise, and that was to give everything I have to my kids. I have. Mitch Bishop thinks Barstow can do more for Chris than public school, but these test scores—" she tapped the papers on her desk "—prove that public school is doing a very good job teaching Chris. *I'm* doing a very good job. And at the risk of sounding conceited, I don't think anyone else could have done better."

"What do you think he'll do when he sees the results?"

Jamie shook her head. "I don't know. We'll just have to wait and see."

"Hi," a masculine voice said when she answered the phone's ring on Friday night. "It's Mitch."

Jamie tried to ignore the way her pulse speeded up at his soft, sexy tone. After all, it had been eight days since he'd said he would try to catch her in a weak moment. Eight days since she'd heard a word from him and three days since she'd sent home the progress reports—not that she was counting.

"I wanted to call and tell you that I appreciate your sending a copy of the test scores home and to thank you for Chris's gift. I would've called sooner, but I've been in Chicago."

"I understand," she said in a tone that strove for normalcy. She hoped he'd say more about the test results; maybe even admit he was impressed and having second thoughts about Barstow, but she was reluctant to push at the moment. It might sound like gloating. Besides, the scores spoke for themselves, and maybe Mitch would want to arrange another conference with her sometime in the near future. "Did you have a good trip?" she asked instead.

"Very good. I picked up a couple of private schools back East that want to replace every piece of football equipment they have."

"That's good."

Her thankfulness that the talk was general, not personal, came to an abrupt end when he said, "Yeah, it is. So by way of celebration, Chris and I are going out on the town, and we thought you might want to join us. Ah, ah! Don't say no until you hear what's happening," he said, knowing a refusal was forthcoming. "It's a really big night. Dinner at Burger King, ice cream from Baskin-Robbins and ten dollars of tokens at the arcade. How can any red-blooded American woman refuse that?"

Jamie laughed in spite of herself. The evening did sound like perfect fun for a child...or anyone else who felt young and carefree, something she hadn't felt in a long time. His description of how they would spend the evening lured her with the promise of happiness, laughter and fun. She was tempted. Very tempted.

"It really sounds like fun...."

"It will be."

"I'm sorry—"

"But I don't go out with students' parents," Mitch interrupted, finishing the refusal himself with her words.

"Yes, but actually, tonight I'm waiting for my brother to call."

He was silent so long that Jamie couldn't tell if he believed her or not.

"What kind of ice cream do you like?" he asked suddenly.

"Why?" she asked, surprised.

"Just curious."

"New Orleans Praline."

"I'll eat a scoop for you," he said magnanimously.

"That sounds...considerate." Jamie was unable to smother a smile.

"That's me. Considerate as hell. So considerate, in fact, that I'm going to let you get back to whatever you were doing. Actually, Chris is hollering about something."

Surprisingly, Jamie found herself hating to hang up. She'd waited every night to see if he would call, and until this moment she'd refused to admit that she'd been disappointed when he hadn't.

"You're sure you're waiting for a phone call?"

"I'm sure."

"Okay, then."

"You guys have fun," she said brightly.

"We will."

To Jamie it sounded like a promise, a promise she was excluded from by her own decree. "'Bye, then."

"'Bye. Talk to you soon."

Mitch hung up, and Jamie sat staring at her receiver for a long time before she cradled it and began her nightly ritual: a frozen dinner, homework and her bath—all very boring with the knowledge of what she could be doing taunting her mind.

At eight o'clock the doorbell rang. When she opened the door, a teenage boy handed her an entire gallon of New Orleans Praline ice cream, with the comment, "Compliments of Mr. Mitchell Bishop."

Jamie took the unwieldy gift to the kitchen, opened the freezer and knew it would never fit. For thirty minutes she scooped the ice cream into smaller containers, uncertain whether to laugh or cry.

"Did you get the ice cream?"

It was Saturday night, and though she'd secretly been hoping Mitch would call, Jamie hadn't really counted on it.

"Yes, thanks." The thrill of pleasure she felt at hearing his voice was diametrically opposed to her repeated avowals not to take anything he said or did seriously.

"You're very welcome."

"You're getting the bill from the gym if I gain so much as a pound," she threatened.

"You ate some, then?"

"Ate some? I filled every plastic container I had and still couldn't get it all into my freezer, so I ate until I was sick." Mitch laughed, and she thought what a nice sound it was. "How was the night on the town?"

"Pretty good, until we got to the arcade." Frustration infiltrated Mitch's even baritone. "Chris didn't understand the tokens. He kept asking me what kind of money it was. He finally got mad when I couldn't explain it and threw them all over the floor. I made him pick them up, but he didn't want to play anything, then."

"I'm sorry," Jamie said. "He must have gotten confused when he saw that it wasn't any money he was familiar with."

"How would he know the difference?"

"We've been working with money at school."

Mitch's voice mirrored his incredulity. "Why would Chris ever need to know about money?"

Jamie couldn't believe her ears. "It's a cold, cruel world out there. What if you sent him to the store with a ten-dollar bill for a sixty-cent cold drink and he came back with forty cents?"

"I'd go in and confront the person at the register."

"You're missing the point. Chris is a sweet kid, but because he's retarded, some people in the world will try to rip him off. I'd like to try to avert that if possible."

Mitch was silent a moment, and then she heard him sigh heavily. "I hadn't thought about it, but you're right. It's a helluva world out there, isn't it, Jamie?"

Unexpected warmth crept stealthily through her when her first name rolled off his tongue in a deep, mellow tone normally reserved for the bedroom...and making love.

"It isn't the world, Mitch," she repeated softly. "It's the people in it."

"Finally."

"Finally, what?"

"You called me by my first name."

She felt herself smiling. "Yes, I guess I did."

"I suppose it was inevitable, since we're becoming telephone buddies," he said. "We couldn't keep things formal forever."

Jamie knew he was chipping away at her reserve and determination. She knew it and also knew there was no way she could—or would—stop him. "No," she said, "I guess we couldn't."

Mitch didn't call Sunday, and Jamie tried to tell herself she didn't care. Monday arrived, cold and cloudy. She hadn't slept well the night before, wondering why he hadn't called, and when the alarm rang, she groped around on the nightstand for it until she knocked it off and broke it. There wasn't one pair of panty hose in her lingerie drawer without runs, no hot cereal in the house and when she was finally ready to walk out the door, she couldn't find her keys. She felt like screaming and crying. It promised to be a perfectly wretched day, and not even the calendar, whose circled date alerted her to the fact that PMS was part of her problem, was any consolation.

It *was* a perfectly wretched day that only got worse when Lester, brave chameleon that he was, finally succumbed to a loving embrace and died in April Stone's hands. Saddened herself, Jamie had wiped the teary eyes and running noses of the entire class. Then, along with the help of twelve sniffling children, she put Lester into a shoe box and took him to a corner of the playground where they could give him a decent burial.

Though it had barely begun, it was a miserable week so far, and when Sam Jeffries summoned her for a conference during her free period, it seemed fitting somehow.

She made her way to his office with a heavy heart, wondering just what it would take to make her feel better, wondering what would become of Chris when he went to Barstow and wondering what would happen to her if she let Mitch Bishop into her life.

Permission granted by Sam's secretary, Jamie entered the spartanly furnished office without knocking. The sound of the door opening shifted his attention from the papers on his desk to Jamie.

"Come in, Jamie," he told her with a broad smile. "Make yourself at home."

"Hi," she replied, settling down onto the cracked vinyl chair opposite him.

Sam raised a mug with #1 Dad on the side. "Coffee?"

"Yes, thanks."

"I'll get it," he told her, rising and going to the coffeepot sitting on a small table in a corner of his office.

"Thanks."

He glanced over his shoulder. "Two sugars, right?"

Jamie smiled, surprised that he'd remembered. Chad had never remembered how she took her coffee. "Right."

When they each had a fresh cup of the fragrant brew, Sam leaned back in his chair and looked at Jamie consideringly.

"Besides being a good friend to Leah, you've done a great job since you've been here, Jamie."

A warm glow of pleasure spread through her. Job? Teaching was much more than a job. Since Chad, teaching was her life. "Thanks. I work hard at it."

"I know you do." One finger tapped the folder he'd been so engrossed in when she came into the room. "I was looking over the results of your last round of testing. What you've accomplished with these kids is nothing short of miraculous."

She shrugged, uncomfortable with the extra dollop of praise. "Sometimes you just get a good group of students."

"I know that," Sam said with a nod. "Teachers can't do anything without potential, but on the other hand, some teachers can be handed potential on a silver platter and not accomplish with so-called normal kids what you have with these."

"Barbara and Patty and four others deserve some of the credit," she said, mentioning the physical education and speech teachers.

"And they'll get it. All my special ed teachers are dedicated, enthusiastic and exceptionally good with these kids, but it's you who comes up with a solution to a problem when no one else can. You're the one who incorporates innovative techniques into your lesson plans. You're the one who holds our special education program together, Jamie. I know it, and they do, too."

A feeling of pride warred with embarrassment. "Thanks, Sam," she said with a weak smile. "The praise is appreciated. It's been a heck of a week."

"Do you think I called you in here just to give you a pat on the back?" Sam said with a laugh. "I could have done that in the hall."

Jamie's brow pleated. "Why did you call me in here?"

"The supervisor of special education position is up for grabs. Gayle Saunders's husband got a promotion, and they'll be moving to Salt Lake City. He leaves almost immediately, but Gayle plans to stay until the end of the school year. She personally told me she'd like you to consider applying for the job."

"Me? Coordinate the entire parish special education program?" Excitement lent a slight squeak to her voice.

"Yes. It's open to any special ed teacher who wants to apply, but having Gayle on your side is a plus, even if the final decision is the school board's."

Gayle Saunders wanted her as a replacement!

"Of course," Sam went on, "it would mean the end of teaching per se, but you'll be teaching teachers how to do a better job."

Jamie's euphoria died a sudden death. Quit teaching? It would be like taking away the very air she breathed. Still, the opportunity was an honor, very likely the highest she could ever reach in her chosen field. She leaned back against the chair and began to twist a strand of her hair. After a moment her eyes met his again. "What do I have to do?"

"They want every applicant to submit a résumé along with a written proposal of what plans they would incorporate into the system. The pay is as good as can be expected with the budget cuts, and the position is in no danger of being done away with. How about it?"

Jamie's lips twisted wryly. "Give me a break. I'd like to think it over."

"Well, don't take too long. You should have the paperwork in no later than the end of the month."

Less than two weeks! With her mind whirling, Jamie stood and started toward the door.

"Where are you going?"

She turned. "Back to my room to think. After all, I have less than two weeks to get things together."

Sam smiled and reached into a drawer for one of his sweet-smelling cigars.

"Sam?"

"Yeah?"

"I'm not sure I want to give up teaching."

He nodded. "I know. You're good at it. The best. But there are other good teachers. What there aren't too many of are people with vision. And that, Jamie Carr, you have in abundance."

Jamie saw the sincerity in his eyes. She sighed and offered him a wan smile. "Thanks, Sam. I'll let you know."

"Don't be a fool! Take it!" was her brother's reaction.

"Whatever you think, baby," her father offered noncommittally.

"Jamie! What a wonderful opportunity!" her mother enthused.

"Are you stupid?" Leah said. "Think of the power!"

No one except her dad understood her hesitancy to leave teaching behind. He knew that the job and her students had been her salvation when Chad left her.

She was still weighing the pros and cons when Mitch called that night. The sound of his voice came as something of a surprise, especially since he hadn't called the night before. But the real surprise was the pleasure that suffused her when she heard him say hello. As strange as it was, she and Mitch *were* forming a tentative sort of friendship via the phone.

"Jamie? Are you okay?" he asked, hearing the hint of despondency in her voice. "You sound as if you just lost your best friend."

Jamie pushed aside her half-eaten sandwich. "I'm fine. It's just that on top of its being a bad day, Lester died."

"What?"

"Lester died, and I had to have a funeral for him so the kids could understand what was happening."

"Who's Lester?" Mitch asked in consternation.

Jamie explained.

"You have had a day, then," he commiserated.

"But that isn't all." Recounting the conference with Sam, she finished by telling Mitch what she'd told everyone else. "It's a great opportunity, and I'm really flattered. I'm just not sure I want to give up the classroom."

"That's understandable, especially since you're so good at it." His unexpected praise warmed Jamie to her toes. "So what does your principal think?"

"He thinks I should go for it. He says," she told him with dramatic intonation, "that I have *vision*."

"I think he's right," Mitch said quietly, recalling the results of Chris's tests and the montage of teaching aids littering her classroom.

Jamie blinked in surprise. "You do?"

"Yes. Look at your classroom. There are a hundred things there you won't find in any other teacher's room. Besides, you care. You care that kids like Chris won't get ripped off by some jerk in a grocery store. You do a good job, and you take that job beyond the classroom. Like talking to me every night about Chris. Do you think I don't know that if it weren't for him, you wouldn't give me the time of day?"

She listened to him with amazement. How could he know all this about her in such a short time? And did this mean he was beginning to agree with her about what was best for Chris?

"Those kids aren't just students to you. They're human beings with rights and privileges just like everyone else. And the thing about you is that you intend to see that they cash in on them all."

Her voice was barely more than a whisper. "I do?"

"Yes. And do you know why?"

Jamie, who was intrigued by his opinion of her—so different from Chad's—wanted to hear it all. "Why?"

"Because you're dedicated. Because you're enthusiastic about life. And," he said with a hint of a smile in his voice, "mostly because you're so darned stubborn." He chuckled. "I think you must *will* them to learn."

Jamie surprised herself by laughing with him. "Maybe I do. But it's important to me."

He sobered abruptly. "I know."

Silence reigned between them, thick with unanswered questions.

"What did he do to you, Jamie?" Mitch said at last, knowing that somehow her break with her ex-husband was tied directly to her dedication as a teacher.

Jamie gripped the receiver tightly. The compassion in his voice brought the sting of tears to her eyes, but she didn't answer.

"What could he have possibly done to give you such an inferiority complex?"

"I don't have an inferiority complex," she denied.

"Not about your work, no. I think you know you're good at that. But your personal life is a different matter. Where's that do or die, gutsy lady when it comes to her personal life? Why do I get the idea that when it comes to a man-woman relationship you think you're a nobody, and *that's* the real reason you won't go out with me?"

One tear slid down Jamie's cheek. She sniffed and brushed it away. "I don't want to talk about it," she said. "Please."

Mitch heard the sniff and knew it was time to back off. Getting to the heart of things would take time. "Okay. We won't talk about it yet."

Hoping to get the subject back on neutral ground, she asked, "You think I should try to get the job, then?"

"You'd be great at it."

"I'd miss the kids."

"But think of how many more you might be able to reach by putting your ideas to work, by infusing the other teachers with your enthusiasm," he encouraged.

"I do have some things I've been wanting to suggest to the other teachers at school, but I didn't really have the authority, and some of them are a little touchy if they even think you're criticizing their capabilities."

"Then here's a chance to do something about it!''

"Maybe you're right. It's something to think about anyway." There was a new warmth in her voice when she spoke. "Thanks, Mitch.''

"It's okay. So, how about going out to dinner Saturday—you, me and Chris—to celebrate the job we both know you're going to get?''

Ignoring his invitation, she said, "I haven't even said I was going to apply!" But something told her she would.

"But you are, aren't you?''

She laughed softly in defeat. "Yes, I guess I am.''

"Then how about dinner?''

The soft, pleading note in his voice beckoned to her. When the silence stretched on, he sighed. "Not this time."

"No. Not this time.''

"Okay, then. Look, I'm going out of town for a few days, which will give you a little relief from my nightly harassment." Low, self-deprecating laughter filtered through the phone lines. "Maybe I'm giving myself a break, too. I think my ego is bruised beyond redemption.''

A part of her scoffed at the idea that anything she said could bruise his ego, yet she felt a sense of loss at the knowledge that he was going away.

You aren't harassing me. I like you to call. She wanted to say it. Wanted to tell him she would go anywhere he wanted, any time. Her woman's intellect told her she could handle another mature relationship, but her heart, the heart that had been trampled in her youth, cautioned her against further pain. She'd like to tell him to call her from wherever he was going, but of course she knew it would be better for them both if she didn't.

"Do something for me, will you?" Mitch said, breaking the silence.

"If I can." Her voice sounded breathless and unsteady even to her own ears.

"Think about me while I'm gone." The request, simple and breathtakingly sweet, fell on her ears like a benediction. Then, before she could think of a coherent answer, he hung up the phone.

Jamie replaced her own receiver and knew there was little doubt that she would do as he asked. As a matter of fact, there was hardly a moment that passed without a picture of him flitting through her mind, hardly a minute that her heart didn't whisper his name.

Mitch hung up and raked his hands through his hair. Dear heaven! She was driving him crazy. Maybe there was some truth to the old saying about wanting something just because you knew you couldn't have it.

And maybe the sun will rise in the west tomorrow.

He roundly cursed the empty room and called himself ten kinds of fool. He'd sworn he'd never again get involved with a woman who was a serious threat to his heart, and now it was beginning to look as if his vows were all for nothing.

With a mocking laugh directed at himself, Mitch went to bed, knowing that in spite of how he felt, he wouldn't stop pursuing her. He couldn't help himself.

Chapter Five

The bottle of whiskey clanked against the glass as Mitch poured a generous amount of the amber liquid. The sound of Chris's sobbing still rang in his ears. Dammit! Mitch slammed the untouched glass of liquor onto the bar and turned away in disgust.

He shouldn't have spanked him. He should have had more control.

He paced the length of the library, berating himself with every limping step he took. Okay, he thought, so Chris had thrown a plate of food across the room, refusing to eat after a pretty heated argument—a great way to spend his first evening home in two days. Then he had kicked Mitch's bad leg. That had been the final straw and had resulted in Mitch's administering the first spanking of his life. What else could he have done? Mitch's own mother would have whaled the daylights out of him if he'd behaved that way.

But Chris was different.

He was different and had to be handled accordingly. But where did you draw the line? How far did you let him push you, and how much was he allowed to get away with because he was retarded?

Mitch raked a hand down his whisker-stubbled cheek. God, he felt terrible! He could still see the shock on Chris's face when he had grabbed him by the arm. Chris had begun to cry with the first swat—hard, racking sobs that contorted his face and loosed a deluge of tears that swamped Mitch with bitter remorse.

Facing the limits of his knowledge, he sank into a chair near the fire and stared at his hand—a hand so much bigger than Chris's—and admitted that he didn't have the vaguest idea how to handle the child. Admitted that he was completely undone by an eight-year-old. There was some sort of altercation almost every night. Over bath. Bed. Food. Chris's stubbornness pitted against Mitch's ignorance about how to handle him led to indecision. That indecision had led to Chris's knowing he could push Mitch, and tonight he'd finally pushed too hard.

Cursing and rising, Mitch climbed the stairs to Chris's room. Earlier, sounds of sorrow had emanated from behind the closed door, sounds that had driven Mitch back to the library in search of amber forgetfulness. But now, thankfully, all was quiet. Chris must have fallen asleep. Mitch breathed a sigh of relief and turned the doorknob.

The lamp beside the bed cast shadows over the room Mitch had redecorated in a football theme just for Chris, who adored anything and everything about the game. Expecting to see his nephew stretched out beneath the covers, Mitch experienced the sight of the empty bed like a slap in the face. Unease raked cold fingers down his spine. He looked at the corner that boasted a shelf full of toys. His worried gaze moved quickly but thoroughly over the rest of the room. Chris was nowhere to be seen.

"Chris ran away this afternoon."

Joyce's voice. When? Two years ago? Panic, an emotion he seldom allowed himself to feel, rose up in him, squeezing his heart with a fist that seemed to shut off his oxygen.

"I found him in the garage, sitting on the mower."

With Joyce's voice ringing in his ears, common sense told Mitch to check the rest of the house first. Maybe he was watching the fish in the aquarium. Maybe...

"Chris!" he bellowed, turning and running to the adjoining room. But Chris wasn't there. To Mitch's dismay, he wasn't anywhere on the second floor, and, if he was anywhere within hearing range, he chose to keep his whereabouts a secret.

Ignoring the throbbing in his leg, Mitch raced downstairs. He almost yanked the living room draperies from their rods in his anxiety to see if Chris was behind them. He searched every room, every hiding place he could think of, with no luck. Finally there was nowhere left but the kitchen.

The heart he thought was crushed to the limit almost stopped beating when he entered the kitchen and saw the back door standing open.

"Oh, God, no!" he breathed. "Not outside in February. No, please."

He ran through the gleaming white kitchen with its abundance of leafy plants and stainless-steel appliances. Reaching the doorway, he cupped his hands around his mouth and yelled, "Chris! Chris! Come home!"

For endlessly long moments he waited for an answer that never came. Then, shutting the door, he turned back to the room and scraped his hands through his hair. Fear, intense and raw, slammed into him. What should he do? Call Karen and Ian to come and help him look for Chris? Call the police? The police department number was listed on the side of the phone along with the sheriff and fire department numbers. Mitch limped to the phone, glanced at the numbers and began to punch one in.

"Hello." The single word wasn't the weary voice of a beleaguered policeman. It was soft and warm and feminine. Jamie's voice. Mitch sagged against the kitchen counter in relief.

He'd called Jamie by accident. Or was it? Had his mind, under pressure, provided her number because something in his subconscious knew that she was the person closest to Chris since Joyce's death? Had something told him that Jamie would know what to do, where to look?

"Hello?" Jamie repeated when he didn't answer. "Who's there?"

The cautious note in her voice finally penetrated Mitch's relief. She must think he was a crank caller. "Jamie. It's Mitch."

"Mitch?" She heard the note of panic in his voice and shivered with a sudden chill. "What's the matter?"

"Chris is gone . . . run away."

"What! What happened?"

The sound of a harsh sigh came through the line. "It's a long story, and I could use some help right now. Can you come over?"

The tormenting thought of any unwanted attraction between herself and Mitch was obscured by her concern for Chris. Her troubled gaze sought the window. It was dark and cold outside. They needed to find him—and soon. "I'll be there as fast as I can."

"Thanks."

"Mitch!"

"Yeah?" His voice sounded tired, discouraged.

"It's going to be all right. We'll find him."

"I hope so."

The agonized words preceded the soft click as he hung up the receiver.

Jamie grabbed her purse and coat and headed for the car. She made the trip to Mitch's in record time and pulled into the driveway, foreboding clutching at her heart. Two police cars cruised the streets, powerful beams of light scanning the neighborhood in wide, searching arcs. Several people—neighbors, probably—were clustered in groups, talking about what had happened.

Mitch must have been watching for her, because the front door opened almost simultaneously with the slamming of the car door. He raced down the front steps and came to a halt a few feet away from her. To Jamie, who'd almost managed to convince herself that he meant nothing to her, he looked wonderful.

Actually, he looked terrible. His hair was rumpled and spiky, as if he'd run his hands repeatedly through it. His attractive face bore a day's growth of beard and the ravages of the past hour. He looked older than when she'd last seen him, and the slight limp she'd noticed at their first meeting was more pronounced. Her concern, which until now had been exclusively for Chris's well-being, reached out to Mitch.

For long seconds neither spoke. Jamie cursed herself for wanting to put her arms around Mitch and comfort him; Mitch drank in her calmness like a thirsting man quaffs a glass of cold water. He wanted to burrow beneath that fluffy white coat and absorb her warmth, to rid himself of the coldness that had encased him since he'd discovered Chris was gone. He wanted to hold her until he drew the confidence she radiated into himself, renewing his rapidly draining reserves.

"I'm glad you came."

Jamie's bones turned to warm honey beneath the intensity of his gaze and the tone—was it need?—in his voice.

"I got here as soon as I could," she said breathlessly, hoping to break the spell holding them both. If someone had pressed her to explain what she was feeling, she would only be able to say that somehow during the last few seconds her relationship—or whatever you called it—with Mitch had undergone some change so subtle that she couldn't put it into words.

Shaking his head as if awakening from a trance, he raked his fingers through his already mussed hair, confirming Jamie's earlier suspicions. "Thanks. I appreciate your coming." He offered her a sheepish grin. "I went to the phone to call the police, but I guess my subconscious kicked in and I dialed your number by mistake."

Jamie shrugged. "It's okay." Cocking her head toward the car just pulling to a stop at the curb, she said, "I see you did call the police. No sign of him yet?"

Mitch scrubbed at his cheek with the palm of his hand. "No. Nothing. Since I called, I've been thinking that maybe you might have some idea of where he might go. You know him better than anyone else."

Before she could answer, two uniformed patrolmen approached, their shoulders hunched against the cold.

"Find anything?" Mitch asked hopefully.

The older of the two shook his head and turned up the furry collar of his coat against the cold night breeze. "I'm sorry, Mr. Bishop. Maybe he'll turn up soon."

"Yeah," Mitch said, sounding unconvinced. "Maybe."

Jamie smiled at the two men. "Hi. I'm Jamie Carr, Chris's teacher."

Both men touched the bills of their hats in reply.

"I thought Ms. Carr might have a better idea of what's going on in Chris's mind than I do," Mitch explained.

Jamie brushed a tendril of hair from her cheek with a gloved hand. "I'm sorry. All I know is that he's wandered off the playground a time or two, when he saw something that caught his eye.''

''My kid has done the same thing,'' one officer said. He scanned the area and the dispersing neighbors. ''Why don't you both go on inside in case he comes wandering back? We'll let you know if we're on to anything.''

''Thanks,'' Mitch said. The two patrolmen went back to their car, and Jamie followed Mitch into the house. He helped her with her coat and hung his sheepskin-lined jacket beside hers on the hall stand.

''You know, I remember Joyce telling me Chris had wandered away from her a few times, but I don't think that's the case here. We had a pretty bad argument about his not wanting to eat dinner. But that's nothing new; we do a lot of arguing over food and bed.''

Jamie smiled. ''I've run into that stubborn streak of Chris's a few times, myself. He definitely needs a firm hand at times.''

''How firm a hand?'' Mitch queried with a weak smile.

''What do you mean?''

''I spanked him.'' He couldn't even look at Jamie as he made his confession.

From his attitude, Jamie correctly assumed he had inflated the punishment into proportions it didn't deserve. ''So? I've given him a swat or two at school.''

Surprise brought Mitch's gaze back to hers. ''You've spanked him?''

She nodded. ''Just a swat on occasion. We have to have written consent, and another teacher has to be present, but we can spank students. I realize it's a controversial issue, even in the home, but sometimes you can't regain control of a class or a student in any other way." She laughed. "Usually all you have to do with Chris is get out the paddle and put it on the desk."

A smile tugged at the corners of Mitch's mouth. "Now that I think of it, Joyce said the flyswatter worked the same way for her."

"Look," she said, "why don't I make us a pot of coffee, and you can tell me about it."

"Coffee sounds like a great idea."

Jamie followed him into the kitchen but at his request sat at the chrome and glass table while he fixed the coffee. Once the tantalizing aroma began to waft through the room, he sat down across from her. "I shouldn't have done it."

"Did you beat him?"

He looked shocked at the mere thought. "Of course not. But Chris isn't like other kids."

"I know that, but I also know that all kids will push you as far as they think they can. Chris is no different in that regard. I've seen him do it with me, and so have the other teachers. Even though these kids are very affectionate and loving, they can also be stubborn and hard-headed, or whatever you want to call it. Sometimes they wind up running a household because parents give in to them when what they really need is to have some limitations set on their behavior."

Mitch dropped his head into his hands. "You didn't hear him crying."

Without monitoring her actions, Jamie reached across the table and clasped Mitch's wrist. It felt warm and hard to her touch. He lifted his head, and his eyes met hers. When he lowered his hands to the table, she released her hold. "Mitch, you didn't do anything wrong by spanking Chris. Crying won't hurt him."

"But being outside without a coat in February will," he said, with a grim set to his jaw.

"True. But he hasn't been out long. They'll probably bring him home soon."

"I hope so." His brief laugh held no real mirth. "I probably wouldn't have spanked him, but the little brat kicked me."

Jamie smiled. "I thought you were limping."

"Yeah. My leg hurts like hell in cold weather anyway, and Chris didn't help it any."

The coffeepot made a definitive sputtering noise. "Sounds as if the coffee is about done," he said, rising to pour it.

"Mitch."

He turned.

"Did Joyce tell you that sometimes these children become completely unmanageable as they get older?"

"No." He turned back to the cabinets and began taking down the cups and saucers with no more concern than if she'd commented on the weather.

From the look on his face, Jamie knew she had added to the burden he already carried, even if his actions said otherwise. But the more knowledge he had about Chris and his problems, the better off he'd be in the long run. Increasing that knowledge was the most useful thing she could do for him.

"Sometimes," she continued, "they have to be... put somewhere. Somewhere where the people are trained to handle them."

"I have some really good almond cookies. A friend sends them to me from California." He headed toward the walk-in pantry as if she hadn't spoken.

"Mitch, you can't ignore the possibilities," she said to his broad back.

He whirled around so fast that she gasped. His face was a mask of pain. "I'm not ignoring them!" he yelled. "I'm trying to cope with them, dammit! All of them!" His chest heaved with each harshly drawn breath. "And right now," he said, "I've about had it up to here." He made a slashing gesture across his throat. His shoulders slumped beneath his blue dress shirt, and he planted his hands on his hips and lowered his head to stare at the tiled floor.

Jamie watched him fight his emotions, knowing he was undoubtedly facing the biggest challenge of his life. Her heart ached for him. She wanted to go to him and put her arms around his lean middle and assure him that he would learn to cope. But she couldn't do that.

He swallowed, his throat working convulsively as he reined in his emotions with visible effort. Then, in control once more, he straightened and looked at her. Was that the sheen of tears in his eyes or a reflection of the overhead lights? He offered her a wan, apologetic smile. "Let me get those cookies."

Jamie responded to his smile with one that matched and rose to pour the coffee into the waiting cups.

"Oh, God!"

The intensity of the throaty words reverberated from the pantry to Jamie, immediately alerting her to the fact that something was wrong. The cup and saucer she was holding clattered to the countertop. Turning, she hurried across the room and skittered to a halt behind Mitch, who stood just inside the pantry doorway. Her gaze followed the direction of his to the small body sprawled on the floor.

Her cry of surprise was loud in the quiet of the small room. Chris! He was so still, so. . .

"Shh," Mitch whispered. "He's asleep."

Taking a closer look, she saw the slight rise and fall of Chris's chest and heard the soft sound of his snoring. Relief washed over her in huge, calming waves. Together, she and Mitch tiptoed closer, kneeling beside the child who had fallen asleep with his hand still inside a potato chip bag. Several crumpled snack cake wrappers were scattered about him, and an opened can of soft drink sat perilously near one elbow.

Jamie was filled with a warm, maternal feeling. Like all children, Chris looked like an angel asleep—an angel who'd just had a cupcake orgy if the wrappers and his icing-smeared face were any indication.

She glanced at Mitch and saw the sparkling of tears on his dark eyelashes. Rough, tough football hero or corporate giant, the real Mitch Bishop, Jamie was learning, had a marshmallow heart.

Knowing he would be embarrassed if she appeared to notice, she busied herself by trying to disengage Chris's hand from the potato chip bag. He stirred and clutched it closer. She eased it and the can of cola aside. Then, with his emotions under control at last and a smile of thanks on his lips, Mitch lifted Chris into his arms.

Chris, irritated at having his sleep interrupted, shook his head and made a sound of protest. When Mitch stood with his tender burden, Chris opened his eyes and stared sleepily up at his uncle. Then, smiling a smile of singular sweetness, he lifted a hand to stroke Mitch's cheek. "Mitz," he murmured drowsily.

The name was spoken with love and, to Mitch, forgiveness. Without a word, he carried Chris through the house. Sleeping, Chris's body was dead weight. Mitch's already hurting leg screamed out against the extra load and the punishing ascent up the stairs to Chris's room. He hardly noticed.

He somehow got the covers back and eased Chris onto the bed, pulling his jeans off as carefully as possible. The child murmured another sleepy protest and turned onto his side, tucking his hands beneath his cheek and falling back asleep in an instant.

The tears he hadn't been able to shed in front of Jamie rolled down Mitch's cheeks, and he dropped to his knees beside the bed. The strong hand that had once sailed passes through the air with enviable ease brushed back a lock of Chris's baby-fine hair. Love, overpowering in its intensity, flooded Mitch. Even though he'd blown it, he had another chance. He rested his tear-damp cheek against the child's.

I might have lost you, Chris. Oh, God, I might have lost you.

The realization that he was beginning to love Chris too much crowded the relief from his mind. Mitch knew Chris was working a subtle spell on his emotions, just as Jamie was skillfully working the magic of her logical persuasion by trying to convince him to leave things as they were.

He'd been doing a lot of thinking since Jamie had come into his life, and he'd come to one conclusion: loving someone—anyone—meant you were vulnerable. Vulnerable meant you were wide open to ridicule, rejection and hurt—something he'd vowed he'd never be again. If he hadn't learned the lesson well enough from his peers growing up, he'd had a harsh review when he nearly married someone who'd loved fame and fortune more than she'd loved him.

He didn't begrudge Chris his love; loving him was the easy part. It was easy to care for a child who looked at you with those smiling, trusting eyes. Hard not to love a child who was mostly pleasant, happy, even teasing. Impossible to "put away" a child who, when the sorrow over your loss became too much, crawled up into your lap, locked his arms around your neck and murmured, "Don't cry."

Dismay at what he'd allowed to happen shuddered through him. He couldn't bear to love and lose again. And he could have lost Chris, as the episode tonight proved. What if he'd fallen into the pool and drowned? What if he'd wandered off, hadn't been found and had frozen to death? What if some crazy who knew Mitch was Chris's guardian had kidnapped him for ransom?

His anger at Jamie when she suggested that he might have to put Chris away had been a defense mechanism against the pain that the truth of the situation brought. He was in danger of caring for Chris so much that losing him would be unbearable, and that fear warred with his tremendous burden of guilt for wanting to get Chris enrolled in Barstow as quickly as possible so that it *wouldn't* happen. It was a catch-22 if ever there was one.

Chris stirred again, and fearful that he'd wake him, Mitch reluctantly stood. He covered the sleeping child with the blankets and stared down at his smudged face.

I couldn't bear losing you after you became part of my life, Chris. I think I'd die.

But if Chris were enrolled in Barstow, that would never happen. It couldn't. The grounds were too well protected. Chris would be safe from the world, from himself. And he, Mitch Bishop, wouldn't have to worry about having his heart broken again. The vulnerable, already hurting part of him refused to listen to the tiny voice in his heart that whispered that it was too late to send him away to put an end to caring for Chris, that Chris was already too big a part of his life and he already loved him too much.

Bending, Mitch dropped a light kiss onto the child's cheek and, turning off the bedside lamp, eased from the room.

Downstairs, Jamie, whose own emotions were a bit frayed around the edges, had cleaned up the evidence of the pantry raid. She had arranged the almond cookies on a plate and had a cup of hot coffee waiting when Mitch reentered the kitchen.

He sat down and reached eagerly for the fragrant brew. "What a night!"

Jamie stirred in her two spoonfuls of sugar. "Is he okay?"

Mitch nodded. "Unless he overdosed on snack cakes," he said ruefully. "How many did he have, anyway?"

"I counted five wrappers."

His laughter was weary, half-hearted. "That's what we were fighting over. He didn't want broccoli and steak. He wanted cakes. And I guess he got them."

"Obviously."

Mitch suddenly set his cup down with a thud. "I'd better let the police know we found him."

"I called, and from the looks of things outside, they've all cleared out."

Mitch relaxed visibly. "Thanks."

They sipped their coffee in silence for a few moments, contemplative in the aftermath of Chris's disappearance.

"I'm not sure I can handle another episode like this."

"I know it's tough on you," she sympathized, "but you'll find your stride with him. It's just going to take time."

"Yeah. Time." He fixed her with a hard look. "Well, Teach, you might find this hard to swallow, with your dedication and all, but I'm not certain I want to find my stride."

Ignoring her surprise and looking almost embarrassed, he continued, "I've done some hard things in my life, but this tops them all. I know you think we've talked this into the ground, but I really believe he'd be better off with people who can relate to him."

"Barstow," Jamie said, knowing intuitively that he'd made a final decision.

"Yes. Barstow." He pushed his chair away from the table and went to the back door. Shoving the curtain aside, he stared out into the night.

"Surely you can tell from the test scores that he's doing very well where he is," Jamie said.

"I know, and I'm impressed." He let the curtain fall into place and turned to face her, settling his weight on his good leg and hooking his thumbs in his front pockets.

Jamie thought he'd never looked more attractive, never looked more male, never looked more vulnerable.

"It's more than what he's learning. I don't know how to talk to him. I don't know if what I say gets through. I'm floundering around like a beached whale, Jamie. And tonight..." He raked his hand through his hair and laughed harshly. "Tonight just brought it all home. I handled things badly and look what happened."

Jamie's eyes were cloudy with compassion and undisguised earnestness. "Mitch, all parents make mistakes with their kids. They all think they've come down too hard at one time or another. Maybe you did, but I'm not convinced of that. What I am convinced of is that Chris loves you. When you carried him upstairs, he felt love for you, not any resentment for what you'd done."

"I hope you're right," he told her, "but that still doesn't change the fact that I'm no good at this."

"Learning to be a good parent is like learning to play football. You don't get good at it without a lot of time and practice."

"Maybe." The pain on his face couldn't be hidden as he asked, "Is what you said earlier true?"

"What?"

"That Chris might become unmanageable."

She nodded. "It's a possibility. These kids are extremely strong. Sometimes they become violent, and parents are forced to...put them away."

He swore and took a gulp of coffee that burned all the way down. "That settles it, then."

"Settles what?"

There was no sign of hesitation on his face, no symptom of vacillation as he said, "Just as soon as Barstow has an opening, Chris will be there. I'm sorry."

Disappointment—expected but painfully sharp anyway—pierced Jamie's heart. Deep down she'd known what his final decision would be, but she'd been hoping for a change of heart. Hearing him voice his decision crushed those tentative hopes and underscored what she already knew: it would take more than what she was capable of to change his mind or his heart.

What really surprised her was his reason for putting Chris into Barstow. Though he felt private schools might be better equipped, the fact that he thought Chris might become too unruly to handle seemed to be a deciding factor. Still, something about Mitch's wanting to get rid of Chris because he was trouble to deal with simply didn't mesh with the picture she was forming of him.

"As I said, that opening could come tomorrow, or next year," she reminded him.

"Yeah. What are you getting at?"

"What are you going to do with Chris until then?"

The stunned look on Mitch's face was almost comical. It was clear that he hadn't thought his decision through. It was almost as if, once he'd made the decision, it was a fait accompli, over and done with. Jamie watched as he assimilated her question, watched

as dismay replaced the surprise. Dismay, and...
anxiety?

Before she could pinpoint the emotion, he stood to
refill his cup. "What do you think I should do until
then?"

"If I were in your shoes, I'd get rid of the full-time
baby-sitter. If you want to keep her on salary for the
times you're away, that's fine, but start taking the responsibility for him yourself when you are at home.
Give him his baths. Let him read to you. Put him to
bed. Do things together, like you did the other night."

Mitch knew that following her suggestions would
only get him in deeper emotionally, yet he was duty-
bound to do the best for Chris that he could. He
heaved a soul-deep sigh. "I can't do it alone. But if
you'll help me—go out with us sometimes, and show
me how to relate to him until I get the hang of it—
maybe I can learn."

Go out with them. Show him how to relate. While
she had no qualms about helping Chris, to agree
would mean frequent contact with Mitch. And that,
considering the attraction she already felt for him,
would be emotional suicide. But did she have a choice?
After her disasters with Chad and Paul, she had vowed
to help troubled children in any way she could—but
with no strings attached to their parents. Wasn't her
goal to help mold kids like Chris to fit into the world?

She looked into Mitch's face. The stress of the last
couple of hours had left its mark. He didn't look like
a threat to her at the moment; he hadn't been a threat
since she'd been here, and that was because their mutual concern for Chris had been uppermost in their
thoughts and actions. If she agreed to help him,

wouldn't it be the same situation? They would be so busy showing Chris the world and ways to relate to it that their efforts would take priority over any attraction they might feel. Jamie's intellect told her her reasoning was sound enough, but her heart told her she was fooling herself.

She looked into his eyes and knew there had never been any doubt about her answer. "All right," she said. "I'll help."

The smile that brightened his face erased the lingering residue of anxiety and concern. His eyes glowed with relief as he said, "Thanks. You won't be sorry. I promise."

Jamie answered his smile with a weak one of her own, hoping he was right. But she kept remembering the old saying that promises, like rules, were made to be broken.

Chapter Six

Mitch wiped his sweaty palms down his slacks and lowered the BMW's heater another notch, even though he knew a case of nerves, not heat, was the culprit. He couldn't remember being this nervous since he'd tried to read in front of the class during his elementary school years.

He was actually taking Jamie out. Since she'd agreed to help educate him about Chris's condition and how to deal with it two days earlier, Mitch had felt like a different person. He wasn't certain which he was happiest over—finding some way to relate to the child who was his responsibility for life and cut down on the friction between them, or finally getting an opportunity to explore the myriad emotions Jamie brought out in him.

Chris had come home from school with a runny nose and a hint of fever, so Mitch felt it would be better if he stayed at home with the baby-sitter. When he'd called Jamie to tell her and suggest that they go out anyway, she'd declined at first. However, Mitch had finally convinced her that he could learn about Chris even if he wasn't with them.

The picture of an unhappy Chris, pouting because he didn't want Mitch to go out again, was etched indelibly into his mind. He knew Jamie was right—he should make more of an effort to spend time with the boy—but because of his ignorance about and inexperience with Down's syndrome, the few things they had done together had ended up in some sort of altercation. But his going out tonight with Jamie was a step toward remedying that situation, wasn't it? Soon he'd be able to compensate Chris for his absences. And lately, well, he'd had to make that trip to the Chicago factory, and when he'd come back, he'd had a ton of work to catch up on—not to mention his efforts to bolster his love life.

Love life. His soft laughter mingled with the humming of the heater fan. His love life was a joke. He'd called a few of his old girlfriends lately, even a few new women who had caught his eye, but once he had them on the phone to make a date, he found himself crawfishing. He wondered why he hadn't noticed that one's voice was so grating, another was perpetually sniping, and one giggled like a simpering virgin straight from the Victorian era, though if her reputation was to be believed, that definitely wasn't the case.

His reasons for not asking them out were as varied as their names and phone numbers, but the long and short of it was that no one had really turned him on in months. Except Jamie.

A street sign captured his attention and cut through his introspection. In a matter of minutes he was pulling into the parking lot of the apartment complex where she lived, and just as she'd said, her car was sitting out front.

He shut off the engine and opened the door, glancing up at the heavens in an attempt to ward off another stab of nervousness. Crystal stars winked saucily from their lofty perch in a sky as black as Jamie's hair. Mitch drew in and expelled a deep, fortifying breath that vaporized in the crisp night air. Then he stood, closed the door and started up the walk.

Jamie dabbed some new, sophisticated, drop-dead-sexy perfume behind her ears, as if the scent were some kind of magical potion that would somehow transform her into the kind of woman worthy of wearing it. The kind of woman Mitch Bishop was used to seeing... the kind who had what it took to change his mind. Agreeing to go out to dinner with him was a mistake, probably the biggest mistake of her lifetime.

Turning, she reached for the hand mirror and checked her hair, which she'd pulled back into a froth of curls that hung down between her shoulder blades and managed, despite the fact that it was technically a ponytail, to look chic and stylish. She made a moue at her mirror image and hoped the new perfume did half what the saleswoman had promised it would.

With a sigh, she turned back to the larger mirror on the vanity, tripping on the toenails of her bear-feet slippers. She assessed herself and—thanks to Chad—

found little pleasure in the pleasing picture she made in her long black skirt and sapphire Paisley blouse. Common sense and adult objectivity told her she was pretty, but just pretty wasn't good enough for a man like Mitch.

What are you hoping for, Jamie? That one spritz of perfume will turn you into someone like...like Chad's first wife? That it will miraculously make you more gorgeous and less clumsy? Well, you're not champagne and roses. You're diet cola and daisies and always will be!

She groaned in dismay at the turn of her thoughts and reminded herself for the hundredth time that how she looked had nothing to do with going to dinner with Mitch. If Chris hadn't gotten sick, it wouldn't even be considered a date.

Remember, Jamie, tonight you're going to try to convince the man that Chris is right where he needs to be, in a familiar, wholesome and loving environment. And for that, how you look is immaterial.

"Right," she said aloud. Her voice sounded convinced, so why didn't her heart feel that conviction? Was it because she believed the old Mary Poppins theory that the medicine went down better with a spoonful of sugar?

She made another face at the mirror and hooked the second of her pearl earrings as the doorbell rang. The sudden sound crashed through her thoughts. He was here.

Bzzzz.

Where were her shoes? A mental picture of the black pumps where she'd stepped out of them two days before flashed through her mind. They were downstairs in the hall. Grabbing her coat and purse, Jamie went flying down the stairs, wondering how she would get through the evening.

She almost made it. She was a mere four steps from the bottom when the oversize slippers tripped her up, and, with a shriek, she tumbled to the floor.

Stunned, she lay on her side, fighting the sick feeling coiled in the pit of her stomach. Then she felt a blast of cold air and looked up. In black slacks, a pearl-gray shirt and a dark jacket and tie, he looked exciting and vital, wealthy and handsome... and totally out of her league. The sick feeling intensified. She had no business pitting her puny reserves against a man who so obviously outclassed her in every way, even if it was for a good cause.

Mitch swung the door shut, his wide eyes taking in the scene before him. Jamie's coat lay in a white puddle next to her. Her black skirt had ridden up, showing nicely shaped legs covered by sheer black stockings now shredded at the knees. Her youthful face was made up with nighttime perfection, and her ebony hair was pulled back to expose her small ears. The blouse she wore was blue with a touch of plum, clingy and ultrafeminine. Two buttons had popped open, exposing a black lace bra and a generous portion of ivory flesh. A small mole that matched the one on her neck tantalized him from the cleft between her breasts.

His gaze moved to her face, where bright color bloomed. She started to move, and a grimace of pain twisted her mouth. Realizing that she might be hurt brought Mitch to his senses. He went to her and lifted her to her feet, steadying her by holding her close to him.

"Are you all right?"

Jamie forced her eyes to his and pasted a false smile on her red lips, battling that old, ingrained sense of inferiority. "I'm fine. It's these darned slippers!"

Mitch glanced down, noticing the outlandish slippers for the first time. He couldn't help smiling. They were totally... Jamie.

"I think my panty hose are gone," she lamented.

Her voice seemed to hold a note of apology. For the state of her panty hose or because she'd fallen? He frowned down at her with a question in his eyes; she looked back at him with eyes a deep forest green. She stirred against him, and Mitch was suddenly and uncomfortably aware of how close her body was to his. She was so slender, so soft. And her perfume, unlike the scent he associated with her, spoke of sultry Southern nights.

Every molecule of his body warned him that prolonged contact with her was dangerous, but he couldn't help wanting to see if he could kindle the emerald fire smoldering in her eyes. Utterly feminine and disheveled, she epitomized danger and desire—a combination guaranteed to intrigue any red-blooded man—and he faced the realization with a calmness he couldn't believe.

He wanted her. Badly.

Jamie looked up into Mitch's brown eyes. She could read his feelings as clearly as if they'd been printed there. He wanted her. Her heart skipped a beat and began slamming against her ribs in a frenzy of awareness and panic. She wouldn't be misguidedly charmed into a man's bed again. So why was she putting her heart on the line by going out to dinner with him? It was crazy. She was wrong for him, just the way she'd been wrong for Chad.

Chad. Jamie clung to the memory of the way he'd hurt her as a drowning person clings to a piece of flotsam. Handsome, smooth, ambitious Chad. Chad, who'd ultimately jerked her heart out of her breast when he'd told her she just wouldn't do as his wife.

The starch returned to her backbone. As long as she kept that memory at the forefront, her heart was safe. Besides, she reminded herself as she tried to stifle her wayward feelings, it wasn't as if this were really a date. She was going out with Mitch to help him understand Chris better. And Chris's well-being was important enough to make her tolerate an evening with an overly confident, sexy male. With her flagging determination bolstered by the memory of her former husband and her renewed perspective of the situation, she shrugged from Mitch's hold.

"Are you all right?"

She nodded. "I'm fine. Just a little shaken. If you'll go on in and sit down, I'll change my hose and be right down."

"Look, I don't mind if you don't feel up to going out." The words were directed at her back.

Jamie turned on the stairs. "I'm fine. Really. Just make yourself at home."

Frowning, Mitch watched her negotiate the remaining stairs. Was she limping a little? He gave a small shake of his head and shoved his hands into his pockets. Then, with a last look at her retreating figure, he wandered into the living room.

The room was decorated with bright, contemporary furnishings, as diametrically different from his as day from night. It was neat but still looked lived in. Jamie's purse rested on a nest of brightly colored cushions that filled one corner of the low-backed sofa. Schoolbooks lay tumbled on the glass coffee table, and a cup with the dregs of what looked like hot chocolate sat beside them. A pair of boots resided near the sofa.

Nice. And, like the ridiculous slippers, definitely Jamie.

Mitch sat down and picked up one of the books. Math. There was also one about family structure. A notebook caught his eye, and he picked it up. Flipping through it, he realized it was a collection of lesson plans. He was reading the small, precise handwriting when he heard her say, "Find anything interesting?"

The sound of her voice brought Mitch's head up. He felt like a kid caught with both hands in the cookie jar. He looked into her eyes and saw that while she was upstairs repairing her outfit, she'd also repaired her composure. This Jamie Carr with the fire in her eyes and the defiant tilt of her chin was the one he was familiar with, the one who intrigued him—not the flustered, almost fearful yet still completely desirable woman he'd picked up from the bottom of the stairs.

He smiled his pleasure. "Just killing time."

A flicker of uncertainty gleamed in her eyes for a moment at that smile. Her voice lost some of its challenge. "It's mostly basic first-grade stuff. I just use a slightly different approach."

Suddenly eager to get on with the evening and see if he could undermine her determination not to get involved, Mitch rose. "I can't wait to hear about it. Ready?"

A bit taken aback by his sudden change in tactics, Jamie nodded and started to shrug into her coat. He was beside her to help almost instantly, the portrait of a perfect Southern gentleman. It was a picture that was shattered when she turned to face him and saw the blatant desire in his eyes. Jamie licked her lips—an action she regretted when Mitch unwittingly copied it—and turned away. It was almost as if he were *tasting* her. The fluttering of a thousand nervous butterflies started inside her. Excitement battled her common sense as one thing became suddenly crystal clear: she'd been a fool to accept his invitation, Chris or no Chris.

He took her to a small hole-in-the-wall type of establishment unlike anything Jamie would have thought he'd frequent. But, contrary to its outer appearance, the inside was clean, cheerfully decorated and bursting with wonderful smells. Catering to those who had loved Cajun cooking for the last twenty-two years, before it became trendy, Maman Melancon's also offered some of the best mesquite-grilled steaks in two states for those who preferred more traditional fare.

Jamie compromised and ordered steak and lobster, her favorite but something her teacher's pay seldom allowed. Mitch ordered a crab and Bibb salad and blackened redfish.

With their orders placed and Jamie determined to keep this occasion the business dinner it was supposed to be, she blurted, "Exactly why is it you think Barstow can do more for Chris than public school?"

At that moment the waiter deposited an appetizer of marinated crab claws in the center of the table.

The surprise that had crossed Mitch's face was quickly masked as his white teeth closed over the fleshy part of a crab claw and pulled it clean.

"If you aren't a snob about public school, why are you so dead set against it?" she pushed.

Mitch knew he owed her a straight answer, but the memory of the ridicule he'd once suffered was still strong. Partial truths would have to suffice.

"Public school, because of the sheer numbers of kids involved, can't meet every child's needs. I know that from personal experience." The look on his face told Jamie he had no intention of elaborating. He had his reasons and they were valid, at least to him; ergo, he was right.

"You're right, of course," she said, pleased to see she'd surprised him by agreeing. "Public schools are overcrowded in most instances, the classrooms far too full. But in Chris's case we're talking about smaller, specialized classes and teachers specifically trained to meet the needs of those particular kids."

"As is Barstow."

Jamie sighed. She wanted to throw her hands up in defeat but was saved from further comment by the timely arrival of their entrée.

They were well into the meal, and by mutual silent agreement talk had been pleasant and general, when Mitch said, "I gathered from your lesson plans that you don't cover every subject every day."

When she raised her eyebrows in question, he gave a brief laugh. "Just curious. It has nothing to do with Barstow or public school."

She couldn't fault him for his genuine interest in Chris's curriculum, could she? After all, wasn't she here to help him understand not only Chris but also her teaching methods?

"No. If it takes all day for everyone to read, we take all day. The same goes for teaching them about money, as I explained over the phone the other night. I don't rush them. They can't be rushed."

"I understand." He raised his glass and, offering her a slow smile over its rim, asked, "So tell me, Teach, what made you go into special education?"

Jamie was a bit surprised that he'd turned the conversation to her. Chad and Paul had both been more interested in their careers than hers.

Her soft smile was full of reminiscence. "I always wanted to teach. When I was a little girl, all I wanted to play when school was out for the summer was school."

Mitch smiled again. "A true calling."

"I guess so."

"But why special education? Why not regular classroom teaching?"

"I taught regular classes for a year or so, but I saw the need for teachers in special ed and decided to try my hand at it."

"You really like it, don't you?"

"Yeah," she said, with a glow of satisfaction in her eyes and a slow nod. "I do. I love those kids."

"It shows."

Jamie felt a blush creeping up her throat, as it usually did when she was the recipient of praise or slow, heated perusals. Mitch's warm, coffee-colored eyes caressed the froth of curls tumbling onto her forehead, skimmed the rest of her face and rested for an instant on the pulse that suddenly began to beat double-time in her throat. As if she could stop the telltale sign of her emotions, Jamie's hand moved up and her crimson-tipped fingers pressed against the pulse that was racing out of control.

When his gaze dropped to her breasts, which rose and fell with every ragged breath, she knew there was no doubt that she was in trouble. Her skin burned as if she had a fever, while her insides quaked, icy with fear, except for the core of her femininity, which rebelled against her determination to withstand his charm and was hot and melting, readying her reluctant body for something she knew she could never allow.

Jamie tried to swallow and found that her throat was bone dry. She reached for her wine, and before she could stop it, the expected and dreaded happened. Her fingers brushed the glass, and, without warning, it was lying on its side, the wine making a wet puddle on the pristine white cloth.

"Oh, no!" she cried, plucking the napkin from her lap and dabbing at the spilled liquid at the same time she gave Mitch an apologetic look. "I'm sorry. I'm afraid I'm a little clumsy."

Mitch laughed, a low sound that caressed her with fingers of sensual softness. He leaned forward and covered her hand with the warmth of his. At the unexpected gesture, her eyes met and locked with his. Like his mouth, his eyes smiled.

"A *little* clumsy?" he asked.

Her eyes widened, and her racing heart stopped momentarily. She nodded.

"Let's see…you almost knocked over the bud vase the day I came for Chris's IEP."

"You noticed!" she said in dismay.

His grin broadened. "I noticed, and I'm devastated. I was hoping it was your attraction to me that had you all flustered, and now I find out that it's just natural clumsiness!" He tugged the napkin from her hand and laced his fingers through hers.

Jamie looked at their meshed hands, entranced by the differences she saw there. Her fingers were slender and tipped with long nails coated with Sangria-red polish. Mitch's were broad and blunt, his nails cut short and scrupulously clean. It was a hand that denoted physical strength rather than an overly esthetic personality.

Instead of being entranced with their laced fingers, Mitch was entranced with Jamie's face. The slight tremors in her told him she was as affected by his touch as he was by hers. She was affected, but she was fighting it with everything in her. He needed to look into her eyes, needed to see what was going on inside her. He brushed her knuckles with his thumb, and, as he'd suspected, the action brought her eyelashes winging upward.

Fear. There was fear in her eyes, and for the life of him Mitch didn't know why.

Then, continuing to catalog her clumsiness, he continued. "There was also the notable entrance you made when I arrived this evening."

His teasing tone was lost on Jamie. Hectic color rushed to her cheeks, evicting the dull rose of embarrassment that had been residing there. So much for first impressions. Chad had been right. She simply didn't belong in the world he and men like Mitch lived in.

"You're embarrassed. Why?"

When she didn't answer, he smiled and gave her hand a brief squeeze. "What's to be embarrassed about?"

"You didn't fall down the stairs in front of a relative stranger."

"Neither did you. You'd already fallen when I came in," he teased.

"You're splitting hairs, again," she said, trying to disengage her hand. "I imagine you're used to women falling at your feet."

Mitch allowed her to free herself. He made a pyramid of his fingertips; his eyes smiled at her over the top. He liked the way she'd turned her tumble into a play on words.

"Now, why would you say a thing like that?"

"You're a very visible person in Baton Rouge. Your latest exploits frequently make the society columns—and the grapevine."

"Exploits?" He shook his head. "Funny. I thought they were charity balls, telethons and such."

"Are you trying to say there isn't any truth to those stories about you and all those women?" Jamie asked.

"Are you trying to say you care if there is or not?" he retaliated.

Her mouth fell open. "Of course not."

"What a pity."

Jamie's heart began to pound in her chest. Did he mean he cared whether or not she was interested? "What do you mean?"

"I mean it's obvious that you're devoted to your job, but it's a damn shame to lavish all that caring on other people's kids when you could be looking for a man who would love to be the recipient of at least part of it."

Jamie stared at him, her eyes wide and expectant, her parted lips full and inviting as she contemplated his statement.

"Mitch! I told Karen it looked like you sitting here!"

The decidedly British masculine voice brought both Mitch's and Jamie's heads around. A tall, elegant man and a beautiful blond woman were approaching the table.

Jamie thought she heard Mitch swear beneath his breath, but when she turned to him with a questioning look, all she saw was a smile of welcome. He stood, his hand extended.

"Hello, Ian. Good to see you."

The two men shook hands, and the sandy-haired man's slow, attractive smile made his brilliant blue eyes glow. "And you, Mitchell," he said warmly.

Mitch turned his attention to Ian's partner, a woman whose casual elegance, even though she was obviously pregnant, made Jamie green with envy. "Hello, Karen."

The blonde's mouth curved upward into a smile that dimpled her cheeks before she stood on tiptoe and pressed a kiss to Mitch's smoothly shaven face. "Hey, cuz," she said.

Karen was obviously very American.

Mitch held his hand out toward Jamie. "Ian, Karen, I'd like you to meet Jamie Carr, Chris's teacher. Jamie, this is my cousin, Karen Forrest, and her husband, Ian."

"So this is the schoolmarm you were telling me about!" Ian said, his eyes filled with wicked glee. "No wonder she had you in such a tailspin."

What did Ian Forrest mean? Jamie flicked a glance at Mitch and saw him frown at Ian. She shook hands with the newcomers, and Mitch asked them to join him and Jamie for a final cup of coffee. To Jamie's dismay, the couple agreed. She would rather spar with Mitch all evening than be forced to make conversation with these obviously classy strangers. Her marriage had taught her well not to attempt rubbing elbows with the elite.

Karen Forrest tucked a lock of her sleek, chin-length pageboy behind her diamond-studded ear and, resting an elbow on the table, propped her chin in her hand. Her white smile was genuine, friendly. "So you're Chris's teacher?"

Jamie urged a matching smile to her lips. "That's right."

"Jamie's the one who talked me into giving up the tutor and letting Chris go back to public school until there's an opening at Barstow," Mitch explained. "Now she's trying to convince me to let him stay permanently."

"If you don't mind my saying so, Mitchell, my friend, I believe the lady could persuade *me* to do anything."

Jamie felt a sort of panic sweep her. She wasn't used to such easy teasing from handsome, elegant men, and two were definitely more than she could handle with equanimity. Before anyone could respond, Ian fixed her with a friendly leer and gave her an audacious wink. Then he turned to Mitch and said, "Why don't you give the lad a break and leave him where he is, Mitch? Teachers didn't look like Jamie when I was in school."

Karen reprimanded her husband with an elbow to his ribs and a soft "Ian! Be good!"

Leaning over to kiss her temple, he murmured, "Ah, luv, I'm always good, aren't I?"

"Hey, you two," Mitch admonished. "We're in a public place. Break it up, will you?" He wore a long-suffering look as he turned toward Jamie. "They've been married eight years, have two-point-five children and are still nauseatingly crazy about each other."

Jamie forced a thin smile and thought how wonderful that would be.

"So what are you doing after you finish eating?" Ian asked.

Mitch shrugged powerful shoulders. "Nothing special."

"Fantastic! Karen and I are going dancing. Why don't you come along?"

Panic swept through Jamie with gale force. It was one thing to sit across from Mitch Bishop and ward off his teasing banter; it was quite another to have his arms around her.

"Oh, I don't think—"

"Sure," Mitch said, cutting through her objections. "Why not?" He turned to Jamie. The challenging look in his eyes told her he knew she didn't want to go dancing—and why. His voice was as smooth as velvet as he said, "I know you have school tomorrow, but we won't be late."

Jamie stifled a groan, her green eyes filled with irritation. How could she refuse now without seeming like a wet blanket? She nodded her reluctant acquiescence. "All right. As long as we aren't too late."

"Splendid!" Ian said, picking up his cup and exchanging a pleased look with Mitch.

It might have been a trick of the lighting, but Jamie thought she saw Mitch's eyelid lower in a sly wink. She wasn't certain, but she thought what had just occurred was known on the football field as a quarterback sneak.

Chapter Seven

Mitch and Jamie left the restaurant and led the way to the designated club, which boasted a large dance floor and was known for bringing in some of the top entertainment in the country. While Mitch looked for a parking place, Jamie checked the marquee to see who was playing the popular nightspot.

"Ace and the Cobras?" she asked, her tone rich with disbelief.

Laughing, Mitch pulled the car to a stop beneath the glow of an amber light. "Unbelievable, isn't it? They were tops when I was in high school. The nostalgia boom has breathed new life into some of the old groups, and if I'm not mistaken, Ace was always Karen's favorite."

Ian pulled their Mercedes to a halt in the empty space next to the BMW with a squeal of tires, and, laughing at his reckless driving, they all went inside.

The club was dark except for small, clear bulbs like Christmas tree lights that ran around the ceiling and floor and striped the walls at strategically placed diagonals, blinking on and off in sync with the music.

The two couples found a table, and the barmaid, dressed in tight shorts and a white T-shirt emblazoned with the club's name, took their order. A mature Ace, looking even more handsome than he had as a teen idol, blared out a rock tune. Karen and Ian were on the dance floor before the drinks arrived, laughing and gyrating while Ace sang about a bad, bad boy who was crazy about a Sunday-mornin' kind of girl. The Cobras harmonized a doo-wah background while rollicking piano notes danced through the room, electric guitars twanged and the drummer and the crowd tried to raise the roof.

Mitch, who leaned back in his chair, drink in hand, watched the couple on the floor with a smile on his face. Jamie sipped her Brandy Alexander and tried to keep from staring at Mitch. Her real reason for being out with him had faded to the furthermost recesses of her mind. All that seemed to matter was that she was out with him.

No doubt about it, he was attractive. Too attractive. And what was worse, she was attracted to him. She was so caught up in her unwanted feelings for him that she was hardly aware when the band finished the rock song and moved into a slower tune without missing a beat.

"Let's dance."

The words jolted Jamie back to the present. She met Mitch's compelling gaze with confusion-clouded eyes. "Dance?" she echoed.

"Yeah," he said with a smile, his eyes caressing her features with a thoroughness she wouldn't have believed if she weren't experiencing it. "Dance. You know...where we put our arms around each other and move in time to the music?"

"I know what dancing—"

"Come on, then," he said, interrupting her again.

Should she? she asked herself.

No.

Yes.

She would dance one dance and then ask him to take her home. She was utterly confused and ready for this crazy night to end. And she wouldn't be silly enough to accept any more invitations from him unless Chris was along as planned. With her strategy firmly in mind, she nodded and rose. Mitch caught her hand and led her out to the dance floor. When he reached the edge, he pulled her into his arms with one deft movement and began to move in time with Ace's rendition of the old Conway Twitty hit, "Only Make Believe."

Her breath caught in her throat when he rested his cheek against hers, and her first instinct was to put as much distance between them as she could and still be dancing. She pushed gently against his chest.

"Ease up, Teach," he said, pulling her even closer and smiling down at her in the semi-darkness.

Jamie didn't ease up—how could she when her thighs and breasts were pressed intimately against

him? However, short of causing a scene, there was little she could do but finish the dance.

Mitch's arm tightened around her back, a move that
pulled her flush against him. Their forearms were
sandwiched between their bodies, and the back of his
hand rode the gentle swell of her breasts, burning
through the thin silk of her blouse. When his voice,
soft and husky, began to sing in her ear that his only
prayer was that one day she would care, her eyes
closed in a helpless effort to block out the images the
song brought to mind.

Involuntarily she did relax, her breasts melting
against him. Beneath the meager barriers of fabric
separating them, their hearts beat in strong, slow syn-
chronization. His cologne, that musky scent she was
becoming so familiar with, enveloped her in a heady
aura of masculinity. Every shuffling step he took
brushed his thighs against hers. The slight friction was
exciting and kindled a fire deep in the heart of her
femininity, a fire she knew she should fight.

Jamie, lost in a music-induced euphoria, gasped
when someone bumped into them. In his effort to
shield her, Mitch's hand accidentally brushed her
breast. Her body responded nonetheless, her nipple
instantly tightening to pebble hardness.

The sound of Mitch's indrawn breath brought about
her usual embarrassment, and the next thing she knew,
Jamie had lost the rhythm of the music and found her
foot on top of his. She stiffened in his embrace and
came to a complete stop.

"I'm sorry," she said, feeling the threat of tears and
trying to free herself of his hold. Mitch's hand moved
to her shoulders, and he gave her a gentle shake. When

she risked a look at him, he was smiling. The backs of his fingers feathered across her cheek in much the same way they had her breast seconds before. "Stop worrying so much, will you? It's no big deal. I've had my feet stepped on before."

Jamie was silent, beguiled by the glow of humor in his eyes. He smiled. "I'd bet a year's income on one thing, though."

"What?" she asked on a sigh.

One finger moved to trace the contour of her bottom lip. His voice deepened even more. "If that fire I see in your eyes is any indication, I'll wager you aren't clumsy in bed."

It felt to Jamie as if a giant vacuum had sucked all the air from the room, the world, perhaps even the universe. She couldn't breathe, couldn't think, couldn't speak.

Mitch's low, sexy laughter triggered a thousand tingling nerve endings along her spine. She was hardly aware that he pulled her back into his embrace and began to sway with the music once more until she felt the touch of his lips against her ear.

"One thing's for sure, Jamie Carr," he said, his voice holding a hint of promise.

She lifted her head to look at him. "What?"

"I'm damn sure going to find out."

Thirty minutes later, Jamie huddled beneath the covers, wishing the electric blanket would hurry up and do its job. Mitch's confident statement that he intended to find out if she was clumsy in bed had completely undone her. Trembling with emotions she'd vowed never to give in to again, she had asked that he bring her home.

Mitch, realizing too late that he'd gone too far too fast, had agreed. They'd hardly spoken on the drive to her apartment, and when he'd tried to apologize before she got out of the car, she'd thanked him for the evening and hurried up the steps, her back ramrod straight.

Now, shivering from nervous reaction, she admitted that she'd known she was getting in over her head when she agreed to go out with him. She'd known he was the kind of man who was a threat, but she'd ignored her intellect and gone blithely along with his suggestion, telling herself it was for Chris.

Chris. Jamie forced her thoughts from her disastrous evening with Mitch to the child whose well-being was at the root of her misery. Turning onto her side, she punched her pillow and burrowed her face into it. She'd told Mitch she would help him with Chris, and she would, but she had to start thinking about what would be best for her, as well. Deep down, she knew she was fooling herself, but she also knew that fooling herself was the only way she could justify seeing Mitch again.

On Saturday, with the dinner date still fresh in her mind and against her better judgment, Jamie rose early and went with Mitch and Chris to New Orleans, as he'd suggested on Friday. By mutual consent, neither Mitch nor Jamie mentioned the way he'd left her three days before.

The weather was back to typical February standards, a mild fifty-seven degrees that felt even warmer as they drove the eighty or so miles to the famous southern metropolis.

The droves of people milling around the French Quarter in celebration of Mardi Gras, the yearly revelry that would last until Fat Tuesday, must have felt spring in the air if their summery costumes were any indication. With Chris secured between them, Jamie and Mitch looked at antiques—which brought a typical "Yucky!" from Chris—ate *beignets* and drank café au lait until Jamie feared she wouldn't be able to hold the lunch Mitch was promising. Then, because it was something she had always wanted to do, she had her portrait done in pastels by one of the sidewalk artists plying their trade on Jackson Square. Impressed with the results, Mitch had Chris's done, and then, because Chris loudly insisted, Mitch allowed the artist to capture his image on paper.

Jamie watched the picture's progress in amazement. The likeness was uncanny. The artist captured the determination in the angle of his square jaw, the sensuality of his mouth and the warmth in his eyes that drew her unerringly into a web he probably wasn't even aware he was spinning.

After having their portraits done and dining on more street fare for lunch, they went into a small shop that specialized in mask making. Chris, in awe of the marvelous creations, begged until Mitch bought him a bejeweled, feathery concoction that would have put a peacock to shame. They left the shop laughing, Chris wearing his new acquisition with pride.

It was late afternoon when they left the city, tired but content. They were hardly out of the New Orleans traffic when Jamie glanced into the back seat

and saw that the day had exacted a toll for its plea-
sures. Chris was fast asleep, his mask still firmly in
place over his eyes, his face smudged with powdered
sugar from a leftover *beignet*.

Jamie, who was feeling the effects of their exer-
tions herself, relaxed against the seat and basked in the
knowledge that her worries about the trip had been
groundless. She and Mitch had spent the day together
without a single one of those uncomfortable instances of awareness between them. They'd experienced nothing but companionship, camaraderie and
laughter. They were simply two adults bound by a
common goal: to do their best for Chris.

She sighed. It had been a wonderful day, and Mitch
and Chris had both seemed to enjoy it and each other,
proving they could communicate on some levels at
least. She covered a wide yawn, which brought a smile
to Mitch's lips, and settled herself more comfortably
against the seat. All her worrying had been for nothing....

"Hey, sleepyhead, wake up!"

The softly chastising words drew her from a dream
she couldn't remember, a dream that left her feeling
warm and quietly happy inside. Turning toward the
source of the masculine voice, Jamie forced open her
sleepy eyes, and saw Mitch's face close to hers. Very
close. Too close.

She could see the sherry-hued lights in the dark
brown of his eyes and the fine lines fanning out from
their corners. He smiled; the lines deepened, and his
mouth kicked up at the corners in a way that sent her
pulse racing. Definitely too close, she thought, starting to sit up straighter. His hand moved, and, with-

out warning, she felt his knuckles gently stroke her cheek. The unexpected gesture stilled all movement but the erratic beating of her heart.

"Did you know that you talk in your sleep?" he murmured, his touch feathering over the line of her jaw.

Her eyes widened in surprise as the recollection of a kiss—a warm, hard mouth teasing hers to compliance in her dream—leaped to mind. Dusty rose climbed to the zenith of her cheekbones. "I do?"

He nodded and brushed the back of his hand across her heated cheek. "Mmm."

"Wh-what did I say?" she asked, her tongue darting across her lips.

Something very close to a groan escaped Mitch at the unconsciously provocative act. He pushed back a spiral of dark hair. "You asked me to kiss you."

"I did?" Was that husky wisp of sound her voice?

"You did."

His answer was firm and brooked no argument. The teasing look left his eyes, and his hand curved along her cheek. His warm brown gaze plunged into the sea-green depths of her eyes. Latent hunger smoldered in his. Hunger and a need so strong that it was almost frightening. His eyes caressed her boldly, telling her without words what he wanted, letting her see the full scope of his desire. Then the hunger softened, and his eyes caressed every inch of her face, asking permission for something she knew she shouldn't grant. The thoroughness of his perusal left her feeling light-headed, as if she'd drunk too much champagne.

Slowly his head began to lower.

This was no dream. This was real. His nearness triggered another memory from the dream, the feel of his body pressing hers into the softness of a bed, his tongue filling the cavern of her mouth, his body filling...

"No!" Her protest was accompanied by a single negative shake of her head. But it was a soft sound and definitely lacked conviction. Which was why, she thought, as his lips neared hers, he ignored it.

The first tentative touch of his mouth might have been imagined, it was so light. Might have been but wasn't. The jolt of electricity that shot through her told her it was real, not imagined.

His second kiss was gentle, undemanding, as if he was waiting to see if she would stop him. When Jamie didn't, the hand on her cheek splayed wide and winnowed through her hair, cradling the back of her head and drawing her nearer. She moaned a protest and lifted her hands to push him away. But her hands got sidetracked by the breadth of his shoulders, and, moving beneath the bulk of his coat, her palms settled against the warmth of his chest.

Without warning, his hand—that skillful hand that had zinged innumerable touchdowns—closed oh, so gently over her sweater-covered breast. A sound, more of a whimper than anything, escaped from her throat and hung on the air between them for a millisecond before Mitch swallowed it with his kiss.

He might have interpreted it as a sound of her growing need, but Jamie heard it as the first crumblings of the emotional walls surrounding her heart.

A corresponding growl of pleasure issued from Mitch's throat before his mouth opened over hers and his tongue thrust deeply into the moist haven of her mouth. The mind-destroying action seemed to pierce the very core of her femininity. His tongue possessed her mouth with a thoroughness that rocked her determination, while his hand—when had it moved beneath her sweater?—gently caressed the fullness of her breast and his thumb rubbed slow, concentric circles over her pouting, aching nipple.

Casting her good intentions aside, she arched toward him, thrusting her lace-encased breast closer to his touch, while jumbled thoughts whirled through her mind, and emotions she had no business feeling buffeted her body.

Mitch. She wanted him. Desperately. She wanted to feel him inside her, his body stroking away the ache created by his caressing tongue and talented hands. Wanted it but couldn't have it. Shouldn't. In a move of total desperation, she turned her head away from the sensitive, mobile mouth whose kiss stamped her as his.

The heat of his breath grazed her cheek, and Mitch rested his forehead against her temple, his breathing, as he fought for control, a ragged sound in her ear. Jamie tried to put distance between them, but Mitch, exerting the slightest pressure against the back of her head, refused to let her. Their eyes met. Clung.

"Don't try to push me away, Jamie," he said, his thumb rubbing the pebbled hardness of her nipple to an exquisite agony. "And don't try to build any walls between us for something another man did to you, because I won't let you. That was then, and today is all that matters. I'm in your life, and I intend to stay there."

There was no hesitancy in his voice. He had made the announcement; she should accept it. And something told her she would have to, whether she wanted to or not.

Slowly, deliberately, he slipped the lace down, exposing her bare nipple to the heat of his caressing thumb. Desire shimmered in his eyes, and Jamie knew the same emotion filled hers. He bent to kiss her again, and her eyes drifted shut in defeat and expectation. He kissed her sweetly, tenderly and with lingering thoroughness, even while his hand reluctantly left her breast and straightened her sweater.

"Yucky!"

Jamie and Mitch jerked apart like two teenagers caught necking in the living room. Chris lay propped on his elbow in the back seat, his mouth downturned with typical eight-year-old disgust, his eyes glittering behind his feathered mask.

Quickly determining that Chris had been unable to see the liberties she'd just allowed Mitch's skilled hands, Jamie glanced at Mitch in an effort to gauge his feelings. Did he feel as hollow, as needing, as she did? Was his pulse racing out of control? If it was, it wasn't apparent, as she watched him reach out and ruffle Chris's hair. "Yucky, huh?"

A feeling closely related to disappointment flooded her. The last few moments might never have existed for all the awareness of them he showed. Dismay that she'd allowed him to penetrate her carefully constructed defenses pushed aside the throbbing disappointment. She moved closer to the door and pushed her hair from her flushed face.

"Hay-mee hot!" Chris said, seeing the gesture and calling her by his interpretation of her first name. Jamie could hardly complain. After all, it was what he'd heard Mitch call her all day.

Mitch's gaze found hers. That sexy, teasing look she was becoming so familiar with moved with slow deliberation over her face. "Yeah, Chris," he said with a half smile. "I believe she is."

Even though she knew she should be used to his teasing personality, Jamie's eyes widened at the deliberate way he'd given Chris's innocent comment a sexual connotation with nothing but a look and the tone of his voice. She didn't think she'd ever get used to referring to desire in such a casual way.

She forced her embarrassment aside and consigned him to the hottest plains of hell with the narrowing of her eyes. Then she turned to look out the window to get her bearings and was surprised to see that the car sat in front of her apartment.

Thank goodness she didn't have to spend any more time with him! She knew her reactions were less than adult, but she was scared. Scared to death of what she was feeling. She forced a brightness she was far from feeling to her voice. "Well, I really enjoyed the day. It was fun."

"It was fun," Mitch agreed, but she knew he saw through her act. "We'll have to do it again soon."

She gave a slight shake of her head. "I don't think that's a good idea, considering—"

"Considering what?" Mitch cut in. "That I kissed you and you responded?"

His bluntness wiped away the last traces of her embarrassment. "Yes."

They stared into each other's eyes for long moments, Jamie wondering how she could back out of her promise to help him with Chris, Mitch wondering what had happened to make her so afraid of getting involved.

"I wish you'd tell me what he did to you," he said at last, scarcely aware that he was vocalizing his concern.

Jamie felt the sting of tears beneath her eyelids. She had no intention of baring all her old fears and heartaches to him, even if he could make her bones dissolve with a kiss. At that moment she wasn't certain whom she hated the most—Chad for planting her insecurities so deeply, Mitch for bringing them out of hiding, or herself for her inability to shake them.

Ignoring his statement, she turned to Chris, blinking rapidly to keep the tears at bay. "Good night, Chris," she said huskily. "I'll see you Monday."

"Awwight," he said with a smile. Then, without warning, he pulled off his mask and, leaning forward, kissed Jamie on the cheek. Pressing his sleep-flushed cheek to the heat of hers, he intoned mournfully, "Don't cry, Hay-mee."

The empathy was her undoing. She looked at Mitch with devil-ridden eyes, wrenched the door open and leaped from the car. She heard him call her name, but she ignored it and raced up the steps as if the hounds of hell were chasing her.

Thrusting her key into the brass keyhole, she glanced over her shoulder. Mitch wasn't following her. Even as she watched, she saw him reverse out of his parking spot and pull onto the street. Trembling, she took a deep, calming breath and fought back the sting of tears, uncertain which emotion was uppermost in her mind—relief or disappointment.

She unlocked her door, slipped inside and leaned weakly against it. Pulling off her beret, she let it fall to the floor. Then, covering her face with her shaking hands, she let the tears fall in a bitter rain.

Mitch stared at the telephone, his index finger rubbing back and forth across his bottom lip. He'd told Jamie he was in her life to stay, and he meant it, but he still couldn't bring himself to call her. What was it, anyway? Fear that he'd pushed too far and she would withdraw again?

Jamie Carr was a paradox. Part young, coltish girl who was embarrassed by her clumsiness and blushed at the slightest sexual innuendo, part mature, modern woman secure in who she was and what she wanted from life. He found both parts equally intriguing.

He closed his eyes and leaned his head against the chair's high back, bringing to mind, as he had countless times since the day before, the memory of kissing her in the car. When was the last time he'd come across such an honest response? Many women, in keeping with the sexual revolution, seemed programmed. Touch them here, and they moaned. Touch them there, and they touched back.

Jamie's response, grudging as it was, came from the heart. She'd meant it when she'd told him no. Meant it from the mind but had been helpless to stop the conflicting response of her body. He'd been right about the fire he'd seen in her eyes. It smoldered inside her, just waiting for someone to come along and fan those glowing embers to fiery life.

Her mouth was sweet, soft, extremely kissable.

Her hands, when she'd rested them against his chest, had ignited a reciprocal fire in him.

And her breasts...Mitch stifled a moan. Her breast, firm yet yielding beneath his palm, had swelled into his hand, and her nipple had responded to his touch with lightning speed. He'd wanted to taste her, to see if her breasts were as sweet as her mouth, but Chris's presence in the car had never left his mind.

He swore and straightened, leaning his elbows on the desk. He knew she didn't want to get involved. He didn't know if it was just him or whether any man would scare her off. He hadn't wanted to get involved, either. He only knew it had been forever since he'd wanted any woman the way he did her. It would take time. It would take skill. It would take patience. But in the end, there was no doubt in his mind that he could have her.

He ignored the tiny voice within him whispering that it was impossible to possess someone without giving something of yourself. He ignored his heart, which tried to make him see that Jamie was different. He ignored the fear of rejection dogging his heels and, before he could change his mind, pulled the phone nearer and punched out her number.

She answered on the third ring.

"Hi, Jamie. It's Mitch."

"Hi."

Just hearing her brought a sense of rightness to his world, but there was a definite lack of enthusiasm in her voice. "I just called to see if you're...all right."

"Yes."

"Jamie...we need to talk."

"We are talking."

"No. We're exchanging words. There's a difference."

She didn't answer.

Mitch sighed, a sound that spoke of his frustration. "We can't ignore whatever this is between us."

"We can try," she told him.

"I don't want to ignore it. I want to explore it...see where it leads."

"It leads to bed, Mitch," she told him in a harsh voice. "You know it, and I know it. And I won't be used by a man again—with or without a marriage license."

Her anger failed to hide her pain. There it was again. She'd been hurt, and badly. "What did that bastard do to you, Jamie? What could he have possibly done to give you such an inferiority complex?" he growled, furious with the unknown husband.

Jamie gripped the receiver tightly, but she didn't answer. She couldn't, for the tears clotting her throat. "I don't have an inferiority complex," she denied. "I'm just smart enough to realize that you're way out of my league."

"I'm not in a league anymore, remember?" he told her with an attempt at levity.

Knowing that she was losing the battle with herself, Jamie decided that the only thing left was to make Mitch see how hopeless anything between them could be. "I'm not the right kind of woman for you."

"How can you know that? We haven't known each other long enough to make that kind of judgment."

She sighed.

"All I know right now is that I want you."

The words, bold and blunt and exactly what she was feeling for him, surprised her nevertheless. "It will never work," she said miserably.

"Oh, it'll work, all right, Teach," Mitch told her in that sexy bedroom voice of his. "I have a feeling it'll work real well."

The innuendo and the sound of his voice sent a frisson of longing through her. Longing and fear. "I won't have an affair with you, Mitch."

"I'm not asking you to."

"Then what are you asking?"

"To give us a chance to explore what's between us...honestly. Can you do that?"

"I'm not sure."

"You don't think it will work because our life-styles are too different?"

"Yes."

"I don't buy that, and you're a fool if you do. You at least owe me the same opportunity I'm giving you with Chris."

"What's that?"

"The opportunity to try to change your mind, to prove you're wrong."

Jamie knew she should say no, but a thrill of hope scampered through her, momentarily letting her forget the hateful things Chad had made her believe. She knew she should tell Mitch to leave her alone and learn how to deal with Chris on his own. She knew she should; she knew she wouldn't. She wanted someone to break down the barriers around her heart. She was tired of existing in emotional exile. The truth was, she was ready to risk her heart again, whether it brought heaven or heartache.

She laughed, a pitiful, sobbing sound that tore at Mitch's heart.

"All right," she told him. "You can try."

He swallowed hard at the little-girl note of hopelessness he heard in her voice. "What if I start on Saturday? How about dinner?"

But she wasn't ready to rush into anything with Mitch or anyone else. An idea crept into her mind, an idea that would limit just how far things between them could go—at least for a while.

"Why don't you and Chris come over here Saturday? I've been wanting to have Leah and her family over for ages. That way Chris would have some kids to play with."

She was going to introduce him to her friends. He thought that was a good sign, but he also recognized the ploy for what it was. "You're gonna make it hard on me, huh?" he teased. "But, hey! That's okay. I love a challenge. What time?"

In spite of herself, she laughed. "About noon? The weather is supposed to be good, and the kids can play outside."

"Great!" Mitch said. "What do you want me to bring?"

Jamie had visions of grilled hamburgers if the weather was good. The first barbecue of the year. "How about an appetite?" she suggested with a lightened heart.

"We can certainly do that!" Mitch had a feeling that their unusual relationship had just undergone another change. "Look, honey, Chris is yelling for me, and I gotta go. Think about us, okay?"

"Mitch, there isn't any us—"

A sudden humming in her ear told her he wasn't going to listen to any more of her reasoning. And she was suddenly very glad.

Chapter Eight

Saturday dawned bright and sunny. Jamie spent the day cleaning the apartment and fixing what she could of her dinner ahead, including one of her favorite desserts, a layered concoction made with a buttery, nutty crust, caramel custard, cream cheese and whipped cream. It was so rich, so sinfully good that, tongue-in-cheek, it was called Caramel Climax.

She made her dinner preparations, both longing for and dreading Mitch and Chris's arrival. She knew she was probably asking for more trouble than she'd be able to handle. Her body, too long without love, yearned toward Mitch Bishop with an intensity that was frightening, and a secret voice from deep inside whispered that it wouldn't take much to send her already crumbling defenses tumbling down around her.

But even knowing all that, she was helpless to keep him at arm's length, helpless to stop seeing him. She was so torn by conflicting emotions that she was sure only that, with Chris in his custody, Mitch was a prime example of the type of man she'd sworn to stay away from. She realized, too, that he was totally wrong for her in every other way. And she also knew that, despite what she'd told him, it was only a matter of time before she let him make love to her.

She unwrapped another slice of cheese and sighed at the truth that forced itself to be recognized. Facing the reality of the situation allowed a small measure of peace to slip into her heart. As Leah was always saying, she'd simply have to deal with things as they cropped up.

By the time Leah, Sam and their two boys, Darren and Bart, arrived, Jamie had everything ready to top the hamburgers, potato salad chilling in the refrigerator, a pot of baked beans simmering in the oven and sodas, popcorn and chips ready for the boys to dive into. She also had her emotions well in hand.

After grabbing a Coke, Sam promptly made himself at home by flopping onto the couch and propping his feet on the coffee table. Jamie sent the boys outside to refill the bird feeder, and Leah wandered around the apartment, oohing and aahing over Jamie's latest decorative touches, especially her Patrick Nagel poster.

When the doorbell rang, Jamie's heart began to pound, and, wiping suddenly sweaty palms down her jeans, she went to the door and opened it with a tentative anticipation.

Mitch stood on the small porch, the sunshine glinting off the golden highlights in his brown hair, his shoulders looking even broader than usual in the football jersey he wore tucked into faded, skin-tight jeans. She swallowed and refused to let her gaze wander over his lower body.

"Hi," she murmured breathlessly, her eyes glued to his.

"Hi, Hay-mee!" Chris cried, throwing his arms around her with his usual exuberant hug.

Jamie turned her attention to the child who stood beaming up at her. "Hi, Chris. Are you hungry?"

"Mmm," he said with a nod, rubbing his stomach and licking his lips.

While Jamie and Chris said their hellos, Mitch was drinking in the sight of Jamie, all the way from her shining hair caught back with combs to the tips of her toes in well-worn aerobic shoes. He made note of the way her rounded bottom and shapely legs filled out her black denim jeans and the way her sweatshirt, appliquéd with a tick-tack-toe game, failed to hide the gentle swell of her breasts. Though she looked every day of eighteen, she also looked every inch desirable.

He observed the easy camaraderie between her and Chris and wondered if she would ever feel that at ease with him. A sudden pang of something that closely resembled jealousy shot through him, making him realize that he wanted that closeness, too, and that what he felt for Jamie was far more than physical desire.

Somehow, Mitch thought, in between the time they'd been arguing over what was best for Chris and his plans to seduce her, Jamie had turned the tables. In dozens of unobtrusive, subtle ways—the look in her eyes, the way she moved, the way she stood up for what she believed in—she had started her own brand of seduction. A seduction of the heart.

He was torn between a quiet exultation and a rapidly escalating fear. He didn't want his heart involved. But on the other hand, he would give up everything he'd worked so long and hard for if only he could be the object of that tender look of love shining from her eyes. He wanted to know her deepest longings, wanted her to share her fears. Wanted to feel her hands on his face, smoothing his hair, touching him....

She put her arm around Chris and turned without warning, surprising a look of longing on his face. The intensity that bound them blocked out every sound in the room. Jamie's eyes widened, and her breath hung in her throat. She fancifully imagined that her heartbeats could be heard by anyone who would stop to listen.

"I'll wager a year's income you aren't clumsy in bed." His words sprang from a place in her mind where she'd told herself she'd hidden them. *"I'm damn sure going to find out."*

Jamie looked back at him, and, to his surprise, Mitch saw no denial or fear in her green eyes. What he did see there defied naming.

Chris pulled on Jamie's sweatshirt and broke the trance binding her and Mitch. Then he tugged again and pointed to Leah's boys, who were coming to check out the newcomers. "Who that?"

"Darren and Bart," she told him, relieved that the tension-fraught moment had passed. "Boys, this is Chris."

Chris waved and cocked his thumb at his uncle. "Mitz."

The Jeffries boys said their hellos.

Jamie wasn't worried about Darren and Bart. Thanks to their parents, they had impeccable manners, and she and Leah had explained Chris's condition to Darren. Bart was only in kindergarten and still at the age where he took people at face value.

"Come on in," Jamie said to Mitch. "I'll introduce you to Leah and Sam."

Leah and Sam were cuddling on the sofa when Jamie and her entourage entered the living room. Leah's face wore a look of unconcealed delight as she took in Mitch's appearance from head to toe. Sam rose and extended his hand, but before Mitch could take it, Chris beat his uncle to the draw, walking across the room with his own hand extended toward Sam and recognition on his face. "Hi. Me Chris. You 'cool?"

Smiling, Sam shook his hand and said, "Hello, Chris. I'm Sam. And yes, I work at school."

Chris indicated Mitch with a slight jerk of his head and said, "Mitz." Then he looked at Mitch, pointed to Sam and said, "Mitz, Ham."

Jamie looked at Mitch, who couldn't hide his amazement that Chris was making the introductions. Smiling slightly, he shook Sam's hand. To Jamie's pleasure, Chris then introduced the rest of the room's occupants to one another. When he was finished and everyone looked her way, she shrugged. "We've been practicing manners at school."

"Figures," she heard Mitch murmur.

"So you're the man behind the Bishop products?" Sam asked.

"Yeah," Mitch said, thrusting his fingers into his front pockets, which was an amazing feat from Jamie's standpoint, since she figured the reason he was late was because he'd had to melt and pour himself into the jeans.

"Good products," Sam said. "I buy them for the boys."

Mitch smiled that slow smile that made Jamie's heart turn somersaults. "That's good to hear."

The two men laughed, and Jamie could tell they would get along just fine. They started to sit down when Leah said. "Ah ah ah. The hamburgers are ready to go on the grill."

Sam groaned, but both he and Mitch dutifully followed the women into the kitchen. Leah handed over the ground meat patties for cooking, with instructions to take the boys outside with them.

"Yes, sweetling," Sam said with mock meekness. "Anything else?"

"No," Leah told him with regal blandness. "That'll do it."

The door had barely closed behind the last child when Leah collapsed against the cabinets, pressed her hand over her breast and said theatrically, "Be still, my heart."

"He is attractive, isn't he?"

"Attractive!" Leah squealed. "They outta ban men like him. I mean, he's a threat to society, for goodness' sake!"

"In what way?" Jamie asked as she took the beans from the oven.

Leah shrugged and started to count off the ways on her fingers. "Heart attacks. Car accidents. Whiplash."

Jamie turned, her brows peaking above questioning eyes. "Whiplash?"

"Yeah. But sideways, you know? From doing a double-take?"

Jamie couldn't suppress her laughter.

"You've changed your mind about him, haven't you?"

"Ouch!" Jamie exclaimed when her finger touched the edge of the hot dish. In a voice as neutral as she could manage, she asked, "What do you mean?"

"You were so dead set against getting involved with him at first, and now you've invited him and Chris into your home to meet your friends. To me, that's tantamount to taking him home to meet your parents."

"Hardly," Jamie said dryly.

"Whatever you say. But you have changed your mind, haven't you?"

"I guess so," Jamie admitted.

"What happened?"

Jamie sighed. This was exactly why she hadn't told Leah before. She was about to undergo a third degree that would make the police force proud.

"Actually, I've been out with him several times. We went to dinner at Maman Melancon's and dancing afterward at Sal's. We spent a day in New Orleans—"

"Dancing!" Leah blurted, interrupting Jamie's story. "You went dancing with Mitch Bishop? He actually had his arms around you?" She sat down. "I can't believe you didn't tell me you've been dating him." She eyed Jamie suspiciously. "Unless you had something to hide..."

A blush she couldn't stop crept into Jamie's face. Leah was too close to the truth for comfort.

"Aha!" she chortled. "Something *did* happen!"

"Nothing happened!"

"What was it? Did he make a pass? Oh, gosh, he did, didn't he?"

"No."

"Yes, he did. I can see it in your eyes."

"What you see in my eyes is anger."

"Pooh! Jamie Carr, you'd better tell me this minute, or I'll...I'll..."

"You'll what?"

"I won't give you my brownie recipe."

Jamie relented with a laugh. She might as well put them both out of their misery and tell Leah what had happened. "Okay, okay, I'll tell you. But no interruptions—agreed?"

Leah nodded and pretended, as Jamie had as a child, to zip her mouth shut.

"We went to dinner and then dancing with his cousin Karen, and her husband, Ian." Jamie paused, recalling the way Mitch's arm had felt around her and the way his body had pressed so tightly against hers. A dreamy look stole across her features. "He's a very good dancer."

"You fell for him!"

Leah's observation snapped Jamie, wide-eyed, from her trance. "No!"

"Oh, yes."

"You're not supposed to be talking," Jamie reminded her, uncomfortable with Leah's observation. She was attracted to Mitch, yes. Strongly attracted. Sexually attracted. But that didn't mean she'd *fallen* for him.

"You told me not to interrupt. I didn't, because you weren't talking," Leah said. "Go on. He did make a pass, didn't he?"

Deciding to throw caution to the wind, Jamie said, "Yes, actually, he did."

"And?"

"And, what?"

"How did it make you feel?"

"Good, Leah," Jamie said bluntly. "It made me feel very good."

"Good grief! You want to sleep with him." The statement was delivered in a complacent tone and accompanied by an I-told-you-so smile.

Jamie turned with a bowl of potato salad in her hands. "It isn't so much that I want to sleep with him," she said consideringly. "It's just that..."

"You want to sleep with him," Leah supplied.

"Yes, I guess so," Jamie said with a laugh. "But it's more."

"Of course it is," Leah said wryly. "It always is."

"Leah!" Jamie said. "Be serious. I'm learning that Mitch is a very caring person who loves Chris a lot. You should have seen him the night Chris was missing and he thought something had happened to him. He was beside himself." She stood in the middle of the kitchen with the bowl still in her hands, a thoughtful expression on her face. "There's only one thing that bothers me."

"What's that?"

Jamie started toward the table. "I get mixed signals from him about why he wants to send Chris to Barstow."

"What do you mean? I thought he was fighting you tooth and toenail."

"He was," Jamie said, setting the bowl on the table and sitting down across from her friend.

"Was? Has he changed his mind about letting Chris stay in public school?"

"No. He's definitely decided to put Chris into Barstow as soon as there's an opening."

Leah whistled. "How and when did all this come about? And why are you still in the picture if he's made up his mind—unless, of course, he wants to sleep with you, too," she tacked on.

Ignoring Leah's last statement, Jamie tried to explain. "Before Chris disappeared, I think I was on my way to convincing Mitch that the public school system was doing a good job. He was genuinely pleased with Chris's progress. But that night, when I explained that he might have to put Chris away at some point in the future, it seemed he made up his mind for Barstow. Since then, there's been no talking to him, no use trying to change his mind. All I've been trying to do is make the time they do have together more bearable for them both."

"Do you think he just doesn't want to be bothered with Chris?"

"I honestly don't know. I do know he wants to do what's best for Chris, and the more I'm around him, I just can't see him as the kind of person who'd put a child in a boarding school just because that child cramped his style.''

''From the little I've seen, I'd have to agree.''

''I think in the beginning he wanted to move Chris because he genuinely believed it was the best thing,'' Jamie said. ''But now, I just don't know.''

''Maybe you can't see the real reason because your own emotions are getting mixed up in this.''

''I've thought of that, and maybe you're right.'' She laughed briefly. ''I swore I wouldn't get involved, and in spite of that, I find myself more drawn to Mitch than I know I should be.''

''Then why do you think you're letting yourself get involved?'' her friend asked sagely.

Shrugging, Jamie got up from the table and went to the refrigerator. Her voice was wry. ''I strongly suspect it has something to do with hormones stirring to life after a very long time and that panic that sets in when a woman comes face to face with the fact that her biological clock is ticking away, she's approaching thirty and there isn't a man on her horizon. I keep telling myself that I should be smarter, that I should remember what life has already taught me, that he's probably no good for me. But when he looks at me, my insides go all fluttery, and when he touches me, I forget all the hurt I've suffered in the past.''

''Good grief!'' Leah said in response to her friend's obvious torment. ''You're in love with the guy!''

Jamie looked as if someone had slapped her. ''I hardly know him!''

''I knew Sam exactly three weeks when we got married, so that isn't valid.''

"I'm not in love with him," Jamie said firmly, but a tiny fear sprouting inside her heart whispered that Leah might be closer to the truth than she wanted to believe.

Leah shrugged. "Whatever you say. But in spite of what good old Chad did to you, he inadvertently did something positive, too."

"What?"

"You came out of that divorce with a lot of strength," Leah said seriously. "And you'd never allow what happened to you back then happen again."

"Come and get it!" Sam yelled, shouldering open the door, the platter of grilled hamburgers held aloft in one palm.

Jamie's gaze was drawn unerringly to Mitch, who preceded the three boys into the room. To her dismay, she saw that he had targeted her with his gaze, as well. To hide the confusion brought on by the heat she saw in his eyes, she turned to the boys and said, "Darren, you sit with Bart and Chris here at the table, okay?"

"Sure."

The boys scrambled into their seats, and Mitch began to fix a hamburger for Chris. "Do you want mustard, Chris?" he asked, a knife poised over the jar.

"No me!" Chris said, with a shake of his head.

"What do you want, then?"

Chris pointed to the jar of mayonnaise and the ketchup bottle. "That. That."

"Say it, Chris," Jamie said.

"No."

"Better let it go," Mitch advised her.

Jamie nodded. He was afraid of starting another scene.

"How about a pickle?"

"Yeah!" Chris replied with a smile.

Mitch smiled in return and put some dill slices on top of the melting cheese. Then he added some potato chips and beans to the plate and handed it to Chris, who began to eat his chips hungrily.

Mitch was talking football with Sam and doctoring his own sandwich when Chris spit a mouthful of hamburger onto his plate and said, "Yucky!"

"Totally gross!" Darren said with enviable nine-year-old nonchalance before taking another big bite of his own sandwich.

Bart giggled and looked at Mitch to see what would happen next.

What Mitch did was blush. "Chris!" he snapped. "Don't do that. It isn't nice."

"Yucky!" Chris repeated, staring back with stoic willfulness. Both Darren and Bart's awed gazes slid from Chris to Mitch.

"Pick up that hamburger, and start eating!"

Jamie saw the stubborn look on Chris's face deepen, saw his mouth turn down at the corners.

Reading the signals of Chris's determination himself, Mitch asked less sternly, "What's the matter, Chris? Why don't you want your hamburger?"

"Mama."

"Mama? We aren't talking about Mama, Chris. We're talking about hamburgers. Now, what's the matter?"

But Chris wasn't talking. He sat there, a familiar stubborn light in his eyes and a look of defiance on his face.

"Okay, tiger, let's go talk this over," Mitch said, reaching toward him. But when he touched Chris, the child twisted free. Taking him firmly by the shoulders, Mitch leaned forward and looked into his face. His voice was soft but firm. "You'd better do as I say, or we're going home."

With a deep sigh and wearing an uncomfortable look, Chris slid from the chair.

"You boys start eating." The command came from Sam after Mitch and Chris had left the room.

"Yes, sir," they mumbled.

Jamie tried to eat, but the anticipation she'd had for the year's first cook-out had disappeared sometime during the last few minutes. Her stomach churned, and her eyes kept straying toward the door. Her ears, suddenly sensitive, were tuned for the slightest noise. Leah's worried gaze moved from Jamie to Sam and back again. The festive mood occupying the room just moments before had vacated the premises.

Jamie was just choking down a bite of beans when Mitch appeared in the doorway, his hair rumpled, his hands on his lean hips. He looked as he had the night Chris disappeared—at his wit's end. "Jamie, can you come in here a minute? I can't understand what he's trying to tell me."

"Sure," Jamie said, blotting her mouth with a napkin and rising from her chair. She followed him into the living room, where Chris sat on the sofa, his arms crossed over his chest and tears streaming down his cheeks.

Her gaze flew to Mitch's face in question.

"I haven't touched him. He's upset about something, and I don't know what it is." His chest expanded with a deep breath, and a soul-deep sigh of frustration wound out of his lungs. "I kept asking him what was wrong, but when he finally did try to tell me, I couldn't understand him."

Jamie nodded and sat down next to Chris. "What is it, Chris? Why didn't you want your hamburger?"

"Mama hih-els," he said.

Jamie glanced at Mitch, who was sitting in a blue chair, his elbows propped on his knees.

"What are hih-els?" Jamie asked.

"Yucky!"

Jamie was beginning to understand Mitch's frustration. She hadn't the slightest idea what Chris was talking about.

"Come and show me," she said at last, standing and holding out her hand. Chris did as she asked, his movements slow, desultory, actions she knew signaled depression. Mitch followed them into the kitchen, and Jamie led Chris to his abandoned meal. She pushed the plate toward him and said, "Show me what's yucky."

Without a word, Chris peeled the top portion of the bun off and pointed to the slices of dill pickle. "Hih-el yucky!"

"He doesn't like the pickle," Jamie said to the group in general. She turned back to Chris. "Why don't you like the pickle?"

He made a face and shuddered. "Mama hih-el. No me."

Realization dawned, and Jamie turned to Mitch with a smile. "These pickles don't taste good to him. They're dills."

The worried look on Mitch's handsome face was replaced with one of tentative relief.

"Elementary," Leah said, with a snap of her fingers.

Just to prove her point, Jamie went to the refrigerator and took out a small jar of sweet pickles. "Is this what you want, Chris?" she asked, twisting the lid off.

He took the jar and smelled them. A brilliant smile brightened his face and rekindled the happiness that usually glowed in his eyes. "Yeah!"

Jamie laughed victoriously and rumpled his hair. "Mama liked dill pickles, but you don't." She looked at Mitch. "When he asked for pickles, he wanted sweet."

"Where Mama?" Chris asked, his smile gone.

The about-face knocked Jamie off-stride. A quick glance at Mitch showed that the shadow of worry was back.

Chris shook Jamie's hand to get her attention. She looked down into his upturned face with the wispy brown hair falling over his forehead and the glittering, slanted eyes that begged for an answer. "Where Mama, Hay-mee?"

A softly uttered curse that betrayed his stress fell from Mitch's lips. He sank into a chair near the table and shot Jamie a look that, like Chris's, begged for help.

She stared back at him. *Why me?*

His face wore a defeated, almost desperate look. *I can't. Please.*

She stood there, torn between a child's need and a man's feeling of helplessness. A helplessness she felt herself. Should she try to explain? It wasn't her place, but, by his own admission, Mitch couldn't always understand Chris or make Chris understand him. A sense of inadequacy, deeper than any she'd felt since Chad had pulled her world out from under her, washed over Jamie, leaving her confused and unsure of how to handle the situation.

What could she say to him? How could she explain death? How could she make him understand, at least in part, that Mama would never come back?

Leah and Sam motioned their boys from the room and silently followed their exit.

"Hay-mee!" Chris whined, vying for her attention. This time he signed the question as he spoke, to make certain she understood. "Where Mama?"

Jamie looked at Mitch again and then back to Chris. She swallowed and asked for divine inspiration. Then, from out of nowhere came the memory of a too still Lester clutched in a small, tight fist. Lester, the valiant chameleon who had given the children so much pleasure, dead from the carelessness of too many clutching hands.

She began to sign and speak at the same time. "Do you remember Lester?" she asked. Chris nodded, and Jamie continued. "Do you remember how he couldn't move, couldn't play anymore after April held him?"

A frown furrowed Chris's brow.

Jamie's fingers flew. "Lester died, Chris. That's what happened to Mama and Daddy. They died."

"A-phril?" Chris asked.

Shaking her head, Jamie went on. "No. April didn't do it. They died in an airplane crash, like on television."

Jamie imagined she could see the thoughts turning around and around in his head like a squirrel in a cage. Finally he began to sign. "Es-ter, botz. Owside." He made a gesture like someone pushing a spade into the ground with his foot, digging. "Mama, Daddy, owside, botz?"

Jamie frowned, trying to make the connection. Ester? Lester. Botz. Digging. Outside. She had put Lester in a shoebox, and the class had taken him outside to give him a proper burial. The frown disappeared as his words meshed and understanding replaced her confusion. Chris wanted to know if his mother and father were outside in a box in the ground—like Lester.

Her throat tightened with unshed tears. What must Chris have thought all this time? Did he think Joyce and Michael had simply gone away? Her heart answered that even though Chris would never fully understand what had happened, he missed his parents, especially when something happened, as it had tonight, to remind him of them.

She blinked back her tears and began to sign and speak. "Yes, Chris. Mama and Daddy are outside in a box, like Lester. But not at school. They're in another place."

They can't play anymore? Chris signed. At the same time he said, "No play?"

Jamie shook her head. "No. They can't play anymore."

"Gone?" he asked in a melancholy voice.

"Yes," she whispered through trembling lips. "They're gone."

"Hay-mee play?" he asked hopefully.

She nodded.

Chris turned his attention to his uncle. "Mitz play?"

Mitch's Adam's apple worked in his throat as he swallowed his own emotion, thankful that Jamie seemed to be succeeding where he hadn't. "Sure, Tiger. I'll play whatever you want."

In another of his abrupt mood changes, Chris raised his fists above his head in a Rocky Balboa sign of victory and smiled from ear to ear. "Awwight, Mitz! Hootball!"

Mitch's answering smile was tired and sad but held a glimmer of relief. "Sure thing, Chris. We'll play football after we finish eating."

As if on cue, Leah's boys burst into the room. From the wide smiles of pleasure on their faces, they must have had their ears glued to the door and heard Mitch agree to play football later.

"Football with Mitch Bishop. Wow!" Darren said, with just the right amount of awe to fortify Mitch's drooping ego. "Just wait till I tell the kids at school!"

"Yeah!" Chris said, his wide smile echoing Darren's enthusiasm. "'Cool!"

Leah ran into the room, her face hot with embarrassment. "Darren and Bart Jeffries, I told you not to come in here. I'm going to put you on bread and water for a week!" She turned to Mitch with a look of apology. "Sam and I went outside for just a moment. I'm sorry."

"Don't worry about it," Mitch said reassuringly. "I think Jamie took care of everything."

Leah indicated Chris with a nod of her head. "Is he okay?"

"He's fine," Jamie said, thankful that it was the truth. She looked around the room at the half-eaten lunches. "Do you think we can salvage this, or should I fix something else?"

"Don't be silly," Leah assured her. "This is fine. Pop the plates into the microwave a minute," she suggested.

Sam entered the kitchen and slid his arm around his wife's waist. "Yeah," he said with a Tom Selleck wiggle of his eyebrows and a definite leer at Leah. "Let's get this behind us and get to the dessert."

Jamie silently thanked him for his attempt to lighten the strained mood lingering in the room.

Leah elbowed him in the ribs. "Sam Jeffries!"

Mitch watched the byplay and felt his good humor returning as thankfulness to Jamie welled inside him. Later he would find a way to tell her how much he appreciated what she'd done. He looked at her, a question in his eyes. "What's so great about the dessert?"

Sam hooted. "What's so great about the dessert? Tell him what it's called, Jamie, my love."

Jamie gave Sam a narrow-eyed look. "It's just caramel custard..."

"Whipped cream..." Leah drawled suggestively.

Jamie made a face at her friend. "Pecans..."

"Tell him what it's called, Jamie," Sam said again.

She cast him a look that sent the corners of his mouth curving upward in a smug smile. Why hadn't she made something else? Who would have believed that Sam would make such a big deal out of an innocent dessert? She forced a look of blandness to her face as she faced Mitch. "It's called Caramel Climax."

Mitch nodded slowly, consideringly. "Caramel Climax, huh? It must be . . . delicious."

She slanted him a glance. "You'll just have to wait and see, won't you?"

"I'm looking forward to it."

She turned away and busied herself with getting a handful of chips. She wanted to ignore the thrill of excitement that tripped down her spine at the look in his eyes that made his innocent statement anything but innocent.

Chapter Nine

Twenty minutes later Jamie and Mitch sat alone at the table. Sam and Leah had taken the boys outside to check out the vacant lot across the street and see if it would do for a playing field. Jamie spooned another mouthful of the caramel confection into her mouth and sighed with both repletion and confusion. Something was wrong with Mitch.

He'd laughed and joked along with Sam about the dessert. The blatant desire in his eyes had sent shivers down her spine. Yet she'd gradually become aware that his laughter was forced and that there was no corresponding happiness in his eyes. And as soon as the rest of the company left the kitchen, his facade of happiness had dropped from him like petals from a dying flower.

Jamie glanced at him and wondered what was the matter. To her surprise she found Mitch's eyes on her. An uncomfortable feeling made her say the first thing that came to mind. "Barbara Chase tells me you won't let Chris run in the Special Olympics."

Mitch took a swallow of coffee. "I've been a sponsor of the event ever since Chris was born. That should be enough."

"That's wonderful, but—"

"Chris isn't running," he said, cutting through her question.

Jamie blinked in surprise. "Do you mind my asking why?"

There was an underlying seriousness, almost a sadness about him as he said, "I don't mind you asking me anything, Jamie."

Warm color suffused her face, but besides embarrassment, Jamie had the strangest feeling she was about to learn something important about Mitch, something that would help clear up the ambiguous signals she'd been receiving from him. "Why won't you let him run?"

"Because I don't want anyone making fun of him."

"Making fun of him! Why would anyone make fun of him?"

There was unrelenting conviction in his eyes as he said, "Because he's retarded, and retarded people are different, and the world at large tends to fear, despise or ridicule anything or anyone that isn't the norm."

Jamie frowned. To a large extent she had to agree, but in educational environments at the very least, times were changing. "It's different now, Mitch. This is the eighties. People don't hide their problems as much anymore. Television commercials offer help for everything from headaches to spouse abuse, illiteracy to alcoholism. They've shown programs, both fiction and documentaries, about everything from teen suicide to mental retardation. No one has to be ashamed of their handicaps or disadvantages anymore. The world is being educated, and the people with disabilities, no matter what kind, are learning that there are others out there just like them. They can find friends. They can get help." Jamie paused, her pleading gaze fixed on his stony face.

"Times may be changing, but human nature hasn't."

She shook her head despairingly and wondered how to reach him. "Chris loves running. He's good at it. Why not let him shine? It would do wonders for his self-image."

"Self-image?" Mitch laughed bitterly. "Funny. That's what I'm trying to preserve."

She jumped to her feet and faced him across the table, indignation sparkling in her jade-green eyes. "Tell me what you're talking about!" she cried, placing her hands palm down on the tabletop and leaning toward him with earnest entreaty.

"If you want me to understand why you're putting Chris into Barstow and why you won't let him run in the Special Olympics, tell me! I'm not a mind reader! I can't understand or sympathize if I don't know the facts! Give me a good reason why you don't want him to run. Give me specifics, damn you!"

Mitch watched her angry tirade in surprise and admiration. This was righteous indignation and determination in its purest form. How could he deny her willingness to try to understand, or even her right to know, especially when she stood there with a hint of tears and pleading in her eyes? Despite the heaviness of his heart, Mitch felt a grudging smile of admiration tugging at his lips.

"You're a helluva woman, Jamie Carr."

She glared at him; Mitch's smile widened.

"I'm dyslexic," he said, deciding to lay all his cards on the table. "So I know all about ridicule." He looked at her consideringly. "Do you have any idea what it's like having people make fun of you because of something you can't do?"

Jamie, Jamie, I guess you'll just never be able to pull off a big dinner party. Jamie, sweets, you just don't have the pizzazz to wear that dress. She recalled Chad's teasing voice in the first few months of their marriage—before the remarks had become cutting, hurting, more accusation than poking fun.

"I dreaded every day of school from first grade on into high school," Mitch confessed. "Reading aloud was a nightmare. You can't imagine what it's like to have a whole class laughing at you."

His words brought to mind another picture from Jamie's past. Herself, wearing the dress she didn't have enough pizzazz to wear, a ruby-red stain from a bumped glass of burgundy splotching the front...and hushed titters of embarrassed laughter at her clumsiness from the other guests.

"That's why I got into sports. I didn't have to be able to read to throw a football," he told her.

The words were like a light bulb going off in her mind, jerking her wandering attention back to the present. She sank slowly back down into her chair.

"That's why you aren't too high on the public school system! You went to public school, and they had no way of knowing you suffered from dyslexia!"

He nodded. "I wasn't diagnosed until my junior year of high school. They only found it then because I had an English teacher who cared."

"Schools are changing, Mitch. Dyslexia was something most teachers weren't even aware of when you were in school. Now they're on the lookout for reasons a child can't read, and kids are put through a whole battery of tests if necessary. I know the system isn't perfect, but it's improving. Just like special education. We have special programs for the high IQ kids as well as the slow learners."

"I understand that. And I've told you what a great job you've done with Chris. But there's more to it than that. For reasons you wouldn't understand, I'm still sending him to Barstow."

Jamie sat there, staring at her empty bowl for several seconds, wondering how they'd come from discussing the Special Olympics to the subject of Barstow—again.

"I want you to teach me signing."

The words were the very last thing she would have expected to hear from him. Unable to hide her surprise, she raised questioning eyes to his face and asked, "Why?"

"Because you were right when you said that I have to deal with Chris until the time he does go to Barstow. Today really brought that home." He scraped a hand through his hair. "I can't get through to him the way you did today."

She offered him a small smile. "Most of that was just lucky questions and the process of elimination."

He shook his head. "I'm not clever enough to play detective like that."

"Of course you are. It just takes patience."

Mitch threw his napkin onto the table with a snort of derision. He rubbed his bottom lip with his forefinger, a gesture she was beginning to associate with thought and uncertainty. "Patience, huh? I'm not long on patience."

"You told me you're persistent," she reminded him.

"I am."

"Isn't it the same thing in the long run?" she asked gently.

He looked into her eyes. They were deep and calm, like the surface of a pond untouched by so much as a breath of wind. There was serenity there, and the confidence he'd admired from the first time he'd seen her. "Maybe it is," he said in a frustration-laced voice. "But I'm telling you, I need all the help I can get."

"I know." Jamie hurt for him. He was being forced to face the fact that Chris was his, now and forever, whether he went to Barstow or not. The boy would always be his responsibility. And that responsibility required a certain amount of selflessness.

"Will you teach me?" The humble quality in his voice sounded out of place with the Mitch Bishop she knew.

Jamie kept her eyes averted and shook her head. "I shouldn't."

Refusing to let her be anything but honest with him and herself, Mitch grasped her chin and turned her to face him. There was evasiveness in her eyes. Evasiveness and a touch of fear. "Why?"

Jamie didn't even try to hide her feelings from him. He knew the battle her emotions were waging inside her. "You know why."

"This has nothing to do with us, Jamie. If you're worried about me making a move, we can have Chris there, too."

She sighed, a harsh sound that spoke of her own frustration. "Let me think about it."

His thumb brushed lightly over her lower lip, then rested at the corner of her mouth. "I'll really work at learning it."

"I know."

And she did. That's what made it so hard. Mitch was changing right before her eyes. She was positive that he wasn't even the same man she'd met that cold winter night. She knew she wasn't the same woman. The knowledge frightened her.

The sounds of Sam, Leah and the kids' laughter filtered through the closed door and reminded Jamie and Mitch that the world still had to be reckoned with. Mitch swore, and Jamie rose and began to rinse the few remaining dishes, stacking them in the dishwasher.

She was so conscious of the approaching group that she didn't hear Mitch come up behind her, didn't know he'd left his place at the table until she felt his hands settle at her waist. The cup in her hand clattered into the sink. Only divine intervention kept it from breaking. He drew her against him, his thighs pressing against the backs of her legs.

"They're coming!" she said in a panicked whisper, tilting her head and looking at him over her shoulder.

"I know." Grasping her upper arms, he turned her around to face him. "Yes or no?"

She knew the question; she knew her answer. The fear of rejection on his face was her downfall. Jamie's throat tightened with the threat of tears. If he was willing to try so hard for Chris, how could she turn down his plea for help?

"Yes," she whispered.

His eyes closed for a moment. Then he opened them and, lifting her wet hands, locked them behind his neck. He pulled her close, his lips meeting hers in a kiss so gentle, so sweet that it stole Jamie's breath... and her heart. The tears in her throat somehow found their way to her eyes, and two fat droplets of moisture trickled down her cheeks.

She had lied to herself and Leah by saying she simply wanted to go to bed with Mitch. Lied in an effort to save herself. She could call it irresponsible. She could call it stupid. But her heart called it love.

"Okay, Chris, when I say, 'Green, twenty-four, hike,' you run out and I'll hand you the ball. Got it?" Chris nodded, and Mitch, who was down on one knee with a hand on Bart's shoulder and one on Chris's, went on. "When I hand it to you, you run down to the goal at the other end and try to keep them from grabbing the hanky out of your pocket, okay?"

"Okay!" Chris said, nodding again solemnly.

Mitch looked at Jamie. "How about you? Got it?"

"Got it."

"Okay, then, let's play!"

Jamie, Bart and Chris spread out on the line of scrimmage, and Jamie, whose mind wasn't really on the game, took her place as center.

Her mind was filled with Mitch and the way he'd looked with something near awe at the two tears she'd shed. His thumbs had brushed them away with excruciating tenderness, and he'd started to say something, but before he could, the boys had burst through the door.

The moment they'd come in, Mitch's mood had undergone another lightning change. Whether the shift was real or forced, he'd been laughing and joking ever since, as if the scene with Chris or their talk had never happened. By the way he was acting, no one would think he had a care in the world. She wondered at his ability to change personas with the same ease Lester had changed colors, but she was beginning to realize that, like Lester's, Mitch's changes were a form of self-protection, a way to camouflage his real feelings.

Still, she could cope with this lighthearted Mitch better than with the serious Mitch, especially since she was still trying to come to terms with the fact that she loved him. It was strange how that one thing changed her whole way of thinking. The weight of the world had been lifted from her shoulders, and she felt truly happy for the first time in ages. Even if Mitch wanted nothing from her but a brief fling, she knew that her love would make the time she spent with him special.

The sexual attraction she felt for him didn't disturb her so much, either. She accepted it as a natural extension of her love and tried to put it out of her mind. She'd deal with that when she had to.

But putting it from her mind was hard. The football jersey Mitch wore accentuated the natural width of his shoulders and the narrowness of his hips. She was tantalized by the heady masculine scent of him and longed to wipe away the perspiration beading his forehead. It seemed that all her senses were conspiring against her, and never more so than when the game had started and she'd found his hands between her legs every time she snapped the ball to him.

"...Green, twenty-four, hike!"

Though she missed the first numbers, the sound of his voice calling out the planned play brought her thoughts back to the game...too late.

"Jamie!" Mitch bellowed as the other team bore down on them. She leaned farther over and, upside down, looked at him through her legs.

"Hand me the ball, dammit!"

Startled, she thrust the ball between her legs and into his waiting hands. She hardly had time to do more than realize—with a bit of a shock—that for one split second his hands were pressed intimately against the most feminine part of her before he was straightening and handing off to a jumping, impatient Chris.

"Run, Chris!" Bart yelled, crossing in front of Mitch to run interference. Chris, who was surprisingly good at zigzagging, made it about three quarters of the way down the field before Darren "tackled" him by yanking the red bandana from his back pocket.

Mitch, Jamie and Bart yelled happily and patted a beaming Chris on the back.

"Hey, you jerks! Haven't you ever heard of a penalty for the quarterback taking too much time?" Sam yelled good-naturedly.

"Yeah, yeah," Mitch said. "But I'm giving my team a pep talk!"

"You can take your pep talks and—"

"Kill the umpire!" Leah hollered, pointing an accusing finger at Sam.

"Umpire?" four masculine voices groaned before they started laughing.

Leah walked over to a grinning Jamie. "What are they laughing at?"

"You don't have umpires in football," Jamie explained. "That's baseball."

Leah shrugged. "Oh. Big deal."

"Okay," Sam said, sobering up with obvious effort as he flung an arm around Leah's shoulders. "Ya'll huddle up!"

"Time!" Mitch called. "I need to have a little talk with my center." Sam flung his hands up in disgust, and Mitch grabbed Jamie's upper arm and led her away from the rest of the players. He moved to stand directly in front of her, planting his hands on his slim hips. "What happened to you out there?"

The memory of his hands touching her came rushing back. "Uh, I, uh," she stammered, shrugging and stuffing her hands into the back pockets of her jeans. "I guess I was just . . . daydreaming."

His eyes made a thorough investigation of the emotions lingering in hers. A hint of embarrassment. A flicker of desire? He recalled her small, sharp gasp of shock when the back of his hand brushed against the juncture of her thighs. His attention had wandered off the game a little, too. A smile as slow and sweet as maple syrup in the spring curved his mouth. He reached out and grasped a lock of her hair, turning the end up and brushing it against her mouth.

Jamie's lips parted the tiniest bit. He wasn't faking this. Obviously he'd worked through his despondent mood.

"Daydreaming, huh?" he teased for her ears only.

"C'mon, you two!" Sam yelled. "Save that stuff for tonight!"

Jamie turned toward the sound of Sam's voice. The slightest pressure of gentle fingers brought her face to face with Mitch once more. "What do you say, Teach? Tonight?"

The heat of his touch and the warmth in his eyes filled her with a breath-stealing need. She moistened her lips, longing to say yes. She'd never wanted to give in so badly in her life, but even though she had acquiesced in her mind, doing so in reality was a different matter entirely. Her refusal was a soft "I can't."

The smile waned; his hand dropped. "Okay. But remember, I'm persistent."

He turned to Sam, Leah and Darren, shrugged his shoulders and held his palms up in a what-can-I-do gesture. "I need a new center!" he yelled. "This one can't get the snap right."

"Me! Me!" Bart screamed, jumping up and down. Smiling broadly, Chris joined in.

"Whoa!" Mitch said, backing up a step. "How about a trade, Sam? I'll trade Jamie for Darren."

"Suits me," Sam said. "But don't you think your team will be a little green?"

"Hey," Mitch said seriously, "don't knock my team. We're young but building. We'll be tough next season. You'll see." He tossed the ball from one hand to the other and turned to Jamie. "Does that suit you?"

Jamie, who was secretly stung by what appeared to be a rejection, could only nod and go to the other end of the field while Mitch started explaining the next play to his team. True to Sam's prediction, Mitch's team goofed again, and Sam, Leah and Jamie were in possession of the ball.

Determined to prove she could play, Jamie kept her mind on the game. Leah made a perfect center, handing off to Sam at just the right time. Sam lobbed a short pass to Jamie who—miracle of all miracles—caught it. She started toward the goal, exultation pounding in her veins. She passed Chris and Bart with a laugh and glanced to both sides. Darren was on her right. Mitch was nowhere in sight. A few more steps and she was home free...

Before she knew what was happening, hands grabbed her jacket and she was jerked backward against a hard body. She heard a soft "Umph!" and the football flew from her hands before she felt herself falling. A voice that must have been hers gave a shrill scream of surprise that mingled with a masculine groan of pain as Mitch twisted in an effort to take the brunt of the fall and, doing so, put the bulk of his weight on his bad knee. The air whooshed from him as he hit the ground and Jamie landed smack dab on top of him.

She could hear whoops and hollers from the boys and groans of dismay from Sam and Leah, but the sounds might have been filtered through three galaxies for all the impact they made. The only thing she was aware of was that her left cheek was pressed against Mitch's chest, and his heart beat out a rapid tap dance beneath her ear. One of his legs was bent at the knee, and the other rested snugly between hers. Her right hand was splayed against the grass at his side, and the other was wedged intimately between his thighs and pinned there by the weight of his denim-clad rear.

Sam saw them and, with a gesture of disgust, motioned for the others to join him on the ground to wait.

Jamie raised her head and looked into Mitch's eyes. Passion's flame glowed in the dark depths, passion and something more. Something that left her trembling with fear and anticipation and need. A gust of wind blew a lock of her hair across his mouth. With their eyes locked, Mitch brushed it aside.

"My hand," she said breathlessly.

He shifted and rolled over, reversing their positions and bringing Jamie's heart to her throat when he rested his weight on his forearms and pushed her hair away from her flushed face. "Are you okay?"

The most masculine part of him was pressed against her thigh, filling her with the most delicious longing she'd felt in years. She could only nod.

A smile kicked up the corners of his mouth. "I'm sorry, honey. I know we weren't supposed to tackle, but I guess all those years of training just...surfaced."

It was hard to believe, she thought, staring up into his handsome face. Hard to believe that one man should have so much going for him. It was also hard to realize that fighting what she felt for him was nothing but an exercise in futility. In an effort to regain control of her runaway senses, her lashes drifted downward to block out the sight of herself mirrored in his eyes.

"C'mon, Teach," he taunted softly. "How about tonight?"

Jamie opened her eyes and, moistening her dry lips, drew in a deep, calming breath that lifted her breasts, pressing their softness more firmly against his chest.

"Okay," she told him with a hint of mischief. "I'll make love with you tonight if you'll let Chris run in the Special Olympics."

The look of surprise on Mitch's handsome face was laughable. He recovered quickly—another trait left over from his football days?—and said seriously, "You know how I feel about that."

A hint of devilry sparkled in Jamie's sea-green eyes. Yes, she knew. That's why she felt so secure in setting the condition. She smiled up at him teasingly. "You're asking me to compromise what I feel is right. Isn't it fair to ask the same thing of you?"

"You little brat!" Mitch said, seeing through her ploy at last. "You only said that because you knew I wouldn't!"

She giggled.

"Well, honey, I've got another deal for you."

Jamie, drunk on the sunshine and Mitch's nearness, threw five years of caution to the wind. "Okay...shoot."

"If you, Sam and Leah win the game, I'll let Chris run in the Olympics. If my team wins, you agree to spend one night with me."

Jamie's mouth opened to protest.

"Just one," he said, holding up one finger.

Jamie thought about the odds. Three adults against one man and three kids. Not bad. She felt pretty confident about agreeing to the bet. "Okay. Deal."

"Deal?" Mitch queried, not believing his ears. "You'll spend the night with me if we win?"

"Yes," she said, "but you're not going to win. We're ahead. We have the better team."

Mitch's mouth curved upward in a cocky grin. "Ah, but you don't have my incentive."

Before Jamie could respond he lowered his head, and his warm, open mouth took hers in a thorough kiss. Making the bet was crazy, she thought, but wasn't it wonderful? Her hand rose and sifted through his hair. Her mouth parted beneath the pressure of his. His tongue made one tentative foray into the secret delights of her mouth when a voice, dripping with little-boy repulsion, rasped, "Yucky!"

Jamie stiffened, but this time Mitch didn't respond with any sign of guilt. Instead he raised his head and looked down at her, a slight smile in his eyes and on his mouth. "Did you ever notice how that kid has a bad habit of interrupting our kissing sessions?"

"I noticed."

"And I notice you two goofing off every five minutes!" Sam said in a wry voice from above them. "What is this, a necking party or a football game?"

Mitch released Jamie and rolled to his back in the new shoots of grass while Jamie raised herself to her elbows. Leah, Darren, Chris and Bart all stood looking down at them with varying degrees of amused censure on their faces. Thank goodness she was among friends!

Darren laughed. "We made a touchdown from your fumble," he told Jamie with a hint of smugness.

"Yeah! Tus-down!" Chris chortled.

"Way to go, team!" Mitch yelled.

"Yeah?" Jamie said, feeling a bit of apprehension flit through her. She rolled to her feet and held out a hand to help Mitch up, the way she'd seen players do on television. "Well, you can bet it'll be your last one!"

She wiped her grass-stained hands on her jeans and started down the playing field. She jumped when she felt someone patting her fanny and turned with a look that teetered between shock and anger.

Mitch drew back his hand and faced her, his palms out as if to ward off a blow. "We guys do that all the time on the football field," he said with counterfeit innocence.

Jamie glared at him.

Sam tried the move on Leah, who rolled her eyes toward the audaciously blue sky.

Darren and Bart agreed with Chris's "Yucky!"

And then they played ball. At the end of an hour the score was twenty-eight to six. Mitch's favor.

Chapter Ten

Jamie looked at the clock, glanced at her reflection in the mirror hanging above the sofa and fiddled with the long tail of the red shirt she wore with her jeans. She sighed and added a log to the fire, her glance making another surreptitious foray in the direction of the clock. Eight-thirty. It had been more than four hours since everyone had gone home. Four hours of wondering if and when Mitch planned to collect on his bet. Four hours of hovering in a suspended state somewhere between anxiety and anticipation.

Would he come? And if he did, would she really let him make love with her? Was she really that foolish?

Obviously she was. She had bathed in a tub full of hot bubbles that were meant to take the chill of nervousness away and had fortified herself with two glasses of her favorite wine. She'd sprayed herself with the sexy perfume again, washed her hair and taken more pains with her makeup than she had in five years—except for the night she had gone out to dinner with Mitch. If those weren't signs of capitulation, she didn't know what was. And besides that, her mind—the only part of her that had remained inviolate to Mitch's charm for so long—had turned on her by filling itself with traitorous imaginings of what making love with him would be like.

Without warning, the doorbell buzzed, shattering her musings and sending her gaze winging to the clock once more. Her teeth caught her bottom lip, and a fearful expectancy filled her heart as she headed for the door.

Jamie's hand closed around the doorknob in a death grip. She turned it slowly, wondering what she would say to Mitch when she opened it, because there was no doubt in her mind that it was Mitch who stood outside her door. Her hand trembled as she pulled it open.

There he was, a single woman's dream, right on her doorstep. He stood directly in front of her, his hands grasping either side of the doorframe above his head, his body blocking out the night. A blue nylon jacket hung open, revealing a black, form-fitting T-shirt with the name *Bishop* stamped on it in white block letters. The shirt was tucked into another pair of those tight, wash-softened jeans.

Jamie allowed her gaze to move slowly back to his face, which had recently been scraped free of any hint of stubble. She could smell the clean scent of his shaving cream and a woodsy no-nonsense soap. Her hands itched to touch him.

Her eyes found his. A hint of a smile lingered there. A bit of a smile and something else. Tenderness? Eagerness? A touch of both? Slowly and deliberately, he placed his hands on her shoulders.

"Hi." His greeting was whisper-soft, his touch whisper-tender.

"Hi," she returned in kind, trying to identify the emotion she saw in his eyes.

She was beautiful, he thought. Not in the classic sense, but to him she was the most beautiful thing he'd ever seen, with her little-girl face painted with big-girl makeup. Mitch stepped through the door, propelling her backward until he could shut it behind them. For just a moment unease flickered in her eyes.

"What is it?" he asked, his hands moving to either side of her neck and tipping her chin back with his thumbs.

"I wasn't certain you'd come."

"I won, didn't I?" he asked, as if that were explanation enough.

She nodded.

"Fair and square?"

"Yes."

"Then why shouldn't I collect?"

Jamie couldn't think of any answer to that, so she said nothing, just looked up at him with troubled green eyes that said clearly, *I'm afraid.*

A half smile lifted one corner of Mitch's mouth, and his thumbs feathered over the slight rise of her cheekbones. "Would you feel better if I told you I'm as nervous as you look?"

"You don't look nervous." Her words sounded shaky and were barely audible.

Without a word, he took her right hand in his and placed it over his heart. He felt warm and firm beneath her touch. And his heart, in direct contrast to his calm demeanor, raced beneath her palm.

The fear in her eyes had lessened somewhat, and Mitch was assaulted with the sudden need to reassure her that everything was going to be all right. "I won't hurt you Jamie. I'd never deliberately hurt you."

Promises. She and Chad had made promises that, in the end, hadn't meant anything—at least not to him.

"Don't!" she cried in a voice bordering on harshness. "Don't make me any promises."

Mitch frowned. "Why?"

"Because if you don't make any promises, you won't have to break them."

"I don't have any intention of breaking them," he told her, realizing the moment the words left his mouth that he meant them. He pulled her into his arms, and of their own volition Jamie's arms slid around his hard middle.

He nuzzled her ear, his tongue tracing the tender shell with thorough deliberation. When he pulled her earlobe into his mouth, Jamie felt the gentle tugging in the most feminine part of her. Her arms tightened around him, and her hips arched toward him in a blatant display of need before she could monitor her response.

The honesty of the simple action stole his breath. His hands tangled in her hair and, with a grip that wasn't hard but wasn't gentle either, pulled her head back until she was forced to meet his gaze. The warmth she usually saw there was magnified a hundredfold. His eyes blazed with hot need.

There was no hesitation in his voice, no compromise as he said, "I want you. More, I think, than I've ever wanted anyone."

Unable to believe what she was hearing, Jamie searched his face, seeking confirmation, confirmation she found. He meant what he said, or he was as good at playing the game of love as he once had been at playing football.

She told herself that just because he said the words didn't mean he meant them for any longer than it took him to possess her. She told herself that just because she saw sincerity in his eyes didn't mean that it would last. But she wasn't afraid anymore. He'd been honest about his feelings, and Jamie knew she couldn't offer him anything less than total honesty herself.

Her eyes mirrored her emotions, and, like the ocean they reminded him of, they darkened while he watched from sea green to a deep forest hue that reflected her inner calm. He knew the subtle change marked the exact instant she made her decision to go through with the bet.

He stood passively while she unlocked her arms from around his waist and wedged them between their bodies, moving them upward in slow increments. Her touch was light, tentative, as if she were afraid he might stop her or worried that she might not be doing the right thing. "Ah...Jamie, honey, that feels so good," he assured her in a voice husky with need.

In thanks, Jamie rose on tiptoe and leaned into him, her mouth finding the hollow at the base of his throat. Daringly, she allowed the tip of her tongue to dip into the shallow indention. Mitch groaned and nudged her legs apart with his knee. His hands slid beneath the hem of her shirt and found the roundness of her denim-clad bottom. Splaying his fingers over her softness, he pulled her closer, wedging his thigh between hers and pressing her aching femininity tightly to him.

She murmured something he couldn't hear, and her head drooped on the slender column of her neck, so that her forehead rested against his chest. Mitch's hand moved beneath the softness of her hair, his strong fingers massaging her nape.

"Look at me, Jamie."

Her head came up slowly, almost, he thought, as if it were more effort than she could make. Their eyes met, Jamie's filled with a slumbering sexuality, Mitch's with blazing desire.

Lowering his head, he took her mouth in a searing kiss that told her without words he was finished with asking permission. To his surprise, her hands moved to the back of his head, and her mouth, like a flower's petals opening to gather sunshine, blossomed beneath his, parting without hesitation for the entrance of his tongue.

She tasted so sweet, he thought. Her mouth seemed to have been waiting for him, saving the nectar of her kisses for him alone. There was an innate innocence about her, regardless of the fact she'd been married before, that fed his desire.

In typical male fashion that all the feminine freedom in the universe would never change, he wanted to be the one to tap that reservoir of sensuality he knew was stored deep within her. Urged by the aching hardness of his own need, his mouth slanted across hers in a grinding kiss, and his tongue stroked the roof of her mouth as he thrust deeper and deeper in a heady dance of desire.

When he could stand no more, Mitch tore his mouth from hers and dragged great drafts of air into his oxygen-starved lungs. The hint of humor in his voice was oddly out of place with the hunger in his eyes.

"I don't want to make love to you in the hallway, but if you don't tell me where the bedroom is, that's what's going to happen."

Jamie understood perfectly well what he meant. A shiver of longing swept through her, a shiver that Mitch misunderstood.

"You're cold."

She shook her head.

"Come with me." He held out his hand, and Jamie placed hers in it. Wordlessly, Mitch led the way to the living room, where the fire burned warmly. He stopped in front of the hearth and bent his head to place a small kiss on her lips while his fingers worked at freeing the buttons of her shirt from their moorings.

Jamie felt his mouth curve upward in a smile against hers. "Why do you wear all these big shirts?" he asked.

"I don't know." Her breath whispered against his mouth.

The last button came free, and Mitch distanced himself from her enough to slide the shirt off. His hungry gaze moved over the ivory flesh of her shoulders, gilded with flickering firelights, and her breasts, covered by a peach-tinted bra that partially hid them from his view.

Her breath caught when his hands moved to the front clasp of her bra, and he freed her breasts from their lacy bondage with one click. Then, without the slightest hesitation, he slid the straps down her arms and sent the bra the same way of her shirt.

Jamie crossed her arms over her breasts in an involuntary act of ingrained modesty.

"Don't," Mitch said, grasping her wrists and anchoring her arms to her sides. "It's a damn shame to hide a body as perfect as yours."

Rose color climbed to perch on her cheekbones.

Mitch smiled. "You'd better save those blushes, Teach. I'm not nearly done with you yet."

Mitch had never considered himself a breast man, but as he feasted on the pretty picture she made standing before him, naked from the waist up, he thought he could definitely get hooked on Jamie's. They were high and firm but not too large. He covered them with his palms and thumbed the rosy au-reole of her nipples, which pouted in instant desire.

"Beautiful," he murmured. "So beautiful."

Her eyelashes drifted shut, and a sigh of contentment escaped her lips. The hardness of her nipples speared his palms and, if possible, puckered more tightly, even as her breasts seemed to swell into his hands. Mitch pressed a kiss through the curls tumbling over her forehead and moved his hands to the snap of her jeans.

Jamie looped her arms around his waist and pressed closer, imprisoning his hands. He kissed her again, a slow, drugging kiss that drained her of coherent thought, of everything but the need to follow the rainbow of pleasure arcing through her. She heard the snap give, a sound that was followed by the slow, downward grating of the metal zipper. With all her senses heightened by the magic of his kisses, Jamie imagined she could hear the giving of each and every tooth.

But the hand that slipped inside the denim and covered the aching mound of her womanhood wasn't her imagination. It was heart-stoppingly, breathtakingly real. As his hand pressed against the silky fabric covering her, his fingers moved beneath the barrier of elastic, unerringly targeting the tiny hidden place of pleasure at the same time his teeth closed with exquisite care over her bottom lip. Jamie tensed momentarily at the unaccustomed invasion, then gave herself up to the almost forgotten feelings of pleasure rippling through her.

Mitch worried her lip with gentle nips and bites for endlessly long moments before he drew it into his mouth with a suckling motion that only enhanced the feelings generated by his stroking, probing fingers. She should stop him, she thought, but she found herself helpless to fight him or the long-dormant need he brought to vibrant life. All she could do was move her hips in rhythm with his touch and go with the flood-tides of passion that swept her heedlessly toward the nearing shores of fulfillment.

Sensing that she was perilously close to losing control, Jamie turned her face away from his bruising kiss and buried it against his shoulder with a soft "Stop."

Mitch refused to do her bidding. "Why?" he asked in a voice that resembled a low purr.

"Because, I . . . ah, Mitch, please . . ." The incoherent murmurings, spoken against his shoulder, were accompanied by the continued movement of her hips.

"Please . . . what?"

Before she could answer, the typhoon of feeling she had hoped to stay hit her, wringing a cry of surprised pleasure from her throat and causing her thighs to tighten around his marauding hand as wave after wave of long-denied feeling buffeted her. She turned her head and blindly sought his mouth, clinging to him tighter and tighter in an effort to hold on to her very soul. She was drowning, spinning, lost. There was nothing to hold on to but Mitch . . . Mitch . . . Mitch . . . .

The soft, whimpering sound of her voice chanting his name was the first thing she heard as the waves lessened to gentle eddies that carried her back to reality. The second thing she became aware of was that one of Mitch's arms was around her while his other hand still touched her intimately. She leaned against him, her lips against his throat, and wished they were on the bed after all. Wasn't it decadent or something to indulge in any kind of sex standing up? the puritanical part of her mind asked.

Sex. She hadn't yet experienced the actual act of loving with Mitch. How much better, more fulfilling would his possession be than what she had just experienced? And heaven help her, if it were any better, how could she stand it? The thought sent her into a sort of panic.

Then, as if he could feel the fleeting bit of tension that passed through her, she felt his lips touch her cheek, her neck, her temple, tasting her with soft, opened-mouthed kisses that somehow soothed.

"I don't think I can take it."

"Take what?" his voice rumbled, his question the first clue that she'd spoken her thoughts aloud.

Jamie leaned back to look at him. "The real thing."

"That bad, huh?" The twinkle of amusement in his eyes told her he knew it wasn't bad at all. Jamie couldn't help the lazy smile that lifted the corners of her mouth any more than she could help the widening of her eyes as his fingers once more started a subtle rhythm.

"Mitch..."

He feathered kisses along her eyebrows, pretending not to hear.

"Mitch. Stop. It isn't fair."

"What?" he asked, the movements stilling as he pulled back to look at her.

She could feel the heat of embarrassment warming her cheeks. "That...that I should...should..."

"Have all the fun?" he asked with that incorrigible bluntness. "You know, I think you're right." He released her and stepped back, pulling his T-shirt from his jeans and over his head.

Jamie blinked. All exquisitely honed muscle, his broad chest and powerful torso were sheathed in golden, sun-kissed skin. While she watched, he kicked off his sneakers and, unsnapping his Levi's, peeled them down his legs. Then he straightened and stood before her in nothing but very brief, very tight, Jockey shorts that did nothing to hide the extent of his arousal.

She elevated her gaze and saw a tenderness in Mitch's eyes that surpassed anything she'd ever seen before on a man's face. Without a word, he dropped to his knees in front of her and reached for the waist-band of her jeans.

"Mitch..." she protested as he began to inch them down her hips.

"Shh... Let me."

He slid the denim slowly down her thighs, past her knees and over her shapely calves. Jamie stepped from them, and Mitch tossed them aside. She felt so bare, so... exposed, standing here in nothing but a pair of skimpy panties. Was she slender enough? Were her thighs firm enough?

"Dear God, you're beautiful."

Clasping her waist, he pulled her closer and closer. His arms circled her hips, and he buried his face in the soft flesh of her abdomen, dipping the tip of his tongue into the small crater of her navel. Jamie arched toward him, her hands sifting through the softness of his hair while his mouth drifted over her stomach, placing random kisses at will, all the time moving inexorably downward. Her legs felt as if they might collapse, and her heart pounded heavily beneath the bareness of her breasts. When he reached the barrier of elastic, he stopped. Then she felt his breath against her as he blew softly along the edge of the fabric that barely covered the tight nest of curls.

The simple, unexpected gesture robbed her legs of their remaining bit of starch, and she sagged against Mitch, completely at the mercy of his sexual exper-tise. "Please..."

Mitch only smiled and gently lowered her to the floor, reaching for a pillow from the sofa to put be-neath her head. He lowered himself onto one elbow beside her and cupped the side of her face with his free hand. His thumb brushed her mouth and skimmed the whiteness of her teeth. Jamie's tongue peeked out and touched the callused skin, curling around his thumb and drawing it into her mouth.

He moved one hand to her breast, his fingers curving around its fullness, while his head lowered and he took her mouth with a punishing kiss. Her mouth opened to his probing tongue, and her legs parted in invitation, an invitation he accepted by moving one leg to rest between hers.

She moaned his name between kisses and arched her hips in a restless search for a closeness he seemed determined to deny. And, just when she thought he would never do it, he transferred his kisses from her lips to her breasts, kissing first one and then the other with a gentle reverence that completely undid her.

Somehow, without ever stopping his kisses, he managed to peel off his briefs and rid her of her panties. He positioned himself between her thighs and waited. Jamie's hand closed around the hardness of his sex and guided him to the moist heat of her. "Mitch..." she said around a sigh.

His answer was a single, slow thrust that elicited a soft sigh of contentment from Jamie. Buried deep inside her, he was still, savoring the moment, trying to assimilate the depth of emotion she brought out in him, trying to fathom the completeness of her surrender, the willingness of her giving. He kissed her temple. "Are you okay?"

"Oh, Mitch," she whispered, pressing a kiss to his shoulder. "I'm fine. Wonderful. It's...more than I've ever..." Her voice trailed away, almost as if she were admitting too much.

"I know." Bracing himself on his elbows, he started a slow stroking with his body.

Jamie matched him thrust for heady thrust, stroke for silken stroke. Mitch murmured love words to her, grated sex words to her, each roll of his hips carrying her toward a height she knew she'd never reached before. Ribbons of shimmering sensation unfurled throughout her.

It was wonderful.

Mitch was wonderful. A perfect lover.

She was crazy, but it was heaven.

What she'd dreamed it would be.

More...

Just a little bit more, and she would be there...

Her breath rasped in her throat; Mitch's was a ragged sound in her ear. She called herself a fool for letting it happen; she prayed it would never end. She was hot, melting, burning, but she trembled in his embrace as though a chill had struck her.

Mitch gave a final, powerful thrust, and pleasure—so intense it was almost painful—exploded inside her. Shock wave after shock wave of delight spread from the juncture of her thighs throughout her body as he emptied himself inside her, chanting her name in a litany of pleasure.

She lay beneath Mitch's weight, savoring the most perfect union she'd ever experienced. Or ever hoped to. She felt whole, perhaps for the first time. The sobering realization pushed aside the lingering effects of his lovemaking and brought to mind things she'd been trying hard to keep from thinking about.

When he left tonight, what would she do? Mitch had asked her to make love to him once—that was the bet. Was once all he would want?

What Mitch wanted was to never move. His hand skimmed the smoothness of her side, the indentation of her waist and recaptured her breast. She was perfect. The most giving lover he'd ever had. Taking things slow had paid off—so well, in fact, that he had no intention of settling for the "once" he'd bargained for. He wanted her every night . . . for forever.

His lips touched her collarbone, and his chest expanded with a deep sigh. He raised his head to look at her, hoping he could see what she was feeling in her eyes. What he saw there was uncertainty.

Opting to take things one step at a time, he forced the teasing tone back to his voice and a smile to his lips as he said, "Wow."

It was impossible not to respond with a smile of her own. "My sentiments exactly."

"That husband of yours must've been nuts," he said offhandedly.

At the casual mention of Chad, Jamie's smile faded and she turned her head away. But this time Mitch had no intention of letting her change or drop the subject. His fingers grasped her chin and turned her back to face him. "Tell me, Jamie. I think after what we just shared I have a right to know why you feel that whatever is between us won't work."

Jamie saw that she couldn't get out of telling him this time, and suddenly she didn't want to. She took a deep breath. "When I met Chad he was divorced with an infant daughter. His wife had left him because he was struggling through school and couldn't give her all she was used to. I came along and fell for him. I married him and became Lisa's mother. A couple of years later, after he got out of school and was climbing the ladder of success, Shelly decided she wanted him back.''

The look on Mitch's face was disbelieving. ''How on earth could he want her after what she'd done to him?''

Jamie's smile held only a trace of bitterness. ''If I recall correctly, he said I wasn't chic, savvy or sophisticated enough to be his wife. The only thing I had contributed to the marriage was that I'd been a good mother for Lisa.''

Mitch swore softly, violently. ''Like I said, the guy must have been nuts.''

''But that isn't all.'' Jamie told him how she'd jumped out of the relationship and almost stumbled into another one with Paul, finishing with the statement, ''That's when I decided that, since I didn't seem destined to find happiness with any man, I'd look for my happiness with the kids I taught.''

''So you completely cut yourself off from men?''

She shrugged. ''I've dated.''

''But never steadily, never anyone you considered socially 'above' you and no one with kids?''

''No. I didn't want to be used anymore for my ability to relate to kids.''

''So what happened with me?''

''I didn't want to get involved, but Chris kept bringing us back together.''

Mitch looked at her, remembering the telephone conversation when he'd told her that he knew if it weren't for Chris, she wouldn't give him the time of day. At the time, he hadn't realized how true the statement was.

Now he understood why she'd turned him down so often and so regularly. He stifled a wry smile. Without knowing it, he'd had two strikes against him going into the game.

But Jamie was wrong about him. He wasn't like either Chad or Paul. But now wasn't the time to tell her. He'd have to show her he cared, prove to her with actions how he felt. He'd have to make her believe that, like her, he hadn't intended to let his heart become involved...but somehow hadn't been able to stop it when it had.

Chapter Eleven

On Wednesday evening, Jamie stared at the blinking cursor on her computer screen and decided that her creativity had taken a trip to some foreign port. Time was running out for getting her presentation together, and all she'd been able to think about since Saturday was Mitch.

When she wasn't thinking about how she had fallen in love with him in spite of all her intentions to the contrary, she was thinking about how wonderful his lovemaking had been. She was smart enough to know she was in over her heart, even if she hadn't been smart enough to prevent it.

With a groan, she rose and began to pace the small room, forcing Mitch from her mind and trying to concentrate on coming up with an idea worthy to land her the job as parish supervisor. But all she could think of in connection with her job was the pickle scene with Chris that had preyed on her mind ever since Saturday—the tears streaming down his face because he couldn't tell Mitch what was the matter and the frustration facing Mitch because he couldn't understand. Obviously, communication was the problem, as it was for most Down's kids and the adults dealing with them.

She sighed. What she needed to do was create a program that would bridge that gap, but all she'd come up with so far was a spin-off of what Mitch wanted to do for himself. A proposal that every special education teacher learn signing to teach to the students and that parents be encouraged to learn it, too, whether through classes at the community college or papers sent home with the child throughout the week.

Sitting back down at the computer, she read the words on the screen for the dozenth time. It was a solid idea, she thought, twisting her hair around her finger, even though it lacked real excitement and would no doubt be controversial. Some would insist that signing was a crutch, that the real need was to concentrate on actual speech. For those, she had her defense ready. She advocated signing not to replace speech therapy or to undermine the work the speech teachers did, but as a means of alleviating the double-edged sword of frustration between adult and child and the limitations on either's ability to communicate.

She heaved another sigh. The idea was valid, yes, but about as exciting as watching dust bunnies collect under the bed.

Glancing at the silver watch circling her wrist, she began to shut down the computer for the night. She was due at Mitch's in an hour for the first of the signing lessons.

She was glad Chris would be there as a buffer between her and Mitch for their first meeting since they'd spent the night together, because she wasn't sure how she was supposed to act under the circumstances. Mitch had flown to Chicago on Sunday morning, and she hadn't seen him since, even though he'd called every day. Although she had admitted her love, that certainly didn't mean he felt the same.

Love. How could she have allowed it to happen? Mitch was rich and handsome—another Chad, another Paul. He was also a man who needed a woman to mother his child. A man who would use her until someone better came along, or until she was used up. Then he would drop her.

Mitch isn't like Chad or Paul. He cares. It was there on his face, in his eyes, no matter what he said. And that was the problem. Should she ignore her head and trust the heart that had proven untrustworthy twice before? Or should she get out while she could still do so with minimal damage to her emotions?

Jamie covered the computer and stood, crossing her arms across her breasts against a sudden irrational chill. She should stop things now, before they went any further, but she knew she wouldn't. Couldn't. Not after Saturday night. There must be something deep within her psyche that was programmed for self-destruction, because there was no doubt that, right or wrong, she was in this thing with Mitch until the end.

* * *

"No, Mitch. Like this," Jamie said two hours later, taking his hand in hers and placing his fingers in the position for P.

After an hour of trying to master the alphabet in signing, there were still several letters he simply couldn't remember or get right.

"Only someone double-jointed could make that," he grumbled.

"Chris can do it," Jamie reminded him with a teasing glance. "And I can do it."

Chris, who had been watching television, heard her speak his name and came sauntering over to see what was going on.

"Show Uncle Mitch how to do P," she said. Chris's mouth turned down, and he gave her a long-suffering look, but he complied with ease.

Mitch turned his hand and laced his fingers through Jamie's. "How do you say *hungry*?"

Without waiting for Jamie to do anything, Chris tapped the tips of his fingers against his chin.

"What is it, Chris?" Mitch asked. Chris repeated the action.

Jamie laughed. "That's how you sign *hungry* or *eat*."

"Yeah? Well, how do I tell her I want pizza, Chris?"

Chris didn't even hesitate before he mimed holding a slice of pizza and pretended to eat it. Then he cocked his thumb at Mitch and said, "Mitz, pi-sa."

Mitch copied Chris's actions for pizza. "I've changed my mind, Chris. I think I want hot dogs," he said with a sly look at Jamie from the corner of his eye. "How do I tell Jamie I want hot dogs?"

Chris pretended to hold a hot dog with two hands, as if he were eating it from one end to the other.

"Like this?" Mitch asked.

Chris's grin spread from ear to ear, and his eyes sparkled. "Yeah!"

Jamie watched for ten minutes as Mitch asked how to sign everything from food to colors to things around them in the room. And as she watched the ease with which Chris actually taught Mitch, an idea began to form in her mind.

She squealed in delight and leaped to her feet, halting the learning game between them.

Mitch smiled at the pleasure on Jamie's face and cast Chris a conspiratorial male look. "She's lost it, Chris."

Chris, who had no idea what Mitch meant, agreed with a nod of his head and a definite "Yeah."

Mitch pulled Jamie down onto his lap. "Whoa! Settle down! May I ask what brought this about?"

Jamie reached out and drew Chris into a loose embrace. She cradled his round face in her hands and brushed the fringe of bangs off his forehead before placing a kiss there. "Thanks, Chris."

"Welcome, Hay-mee," he said politely.

"Jamie..." Mitch began, a threatening look in his eyes.

"I have an idea for my presentation!" she said, flinging her arms around his neck and planting a loud kiss on his cheek.

He looked at her with feigned wariness. "A good one, obviously."

"Yes. A very good one."

"Do you want to explain it before we eat pizza or while we're eating?" he asked.

"Now."

"Me, pi-sa!" Chris cried, rubbing his tummy in a circular motion.

"Overruled," Mitch said, standing and dumping Jamie from his lap onto the floor.

She shrieked with laughter. Pointing her finger at him and pretending anger, she said, "Help me up, you...you..."

"Mitz," Chris supplied.

Jamie fought to suppress a smile. Chris had mistaken her actions for not knowing who Mitch was. "Help me up, you...you...Mitch, you," she said.

Both she and Mitch burst out laughing, and Chris joined in, not wanting to be left out of the fun. Then he grabbed one of Jamie's hands, and Mitch grabbed the other, and they pulled her to her feet, moaning and groaning as if she weighed a ton instead of a mere one hundred and fifteen pounds. Still laughing, they put on their jackets and left the house.

Forty minutes later, Jamie finished her portion of the everything-but-the-kitchen-sink-on-it pizza and the explanation of her idea to Mitch.

"So what you're saying is that the kids themselves—in my case, Chris—would teach the signing to their parents?"

"Yes, and not only to parents, but to kids who don't know it, as well. Of course, a teacher would have to supervise, but I think it would be an invaluable way to utilize the potential in kids like Chris. We could incorporate a way to recognize them with a diploma or something, and it could be a wonderful tool to help them recognize their self-worth."

Mitch lifted her hand from the table and pressed a kiss to her palm. "You and your self-worth hang-ups."

"Problems with self-esteem are at the root of a lot of other problems, Mitch."

"I know," he said, thinking of his own lack of self-worth before football had become his salvation.

"Mitch?" she said, seeing the glimmer of remembered despair in his eyes. "What are you thinking about?"

Mitch dragged his thoughts from the past and focused his attention on the concern on her face. She looked like a serious child, sitting there with her forehead wrinkled and her eyebrows drawn together.

But she wasn't a child, as his body recalled all too clearly. She was a fiery, desirable woman whose slightest touch could set his blood boiling. His eyes caressed her face and lingered on her lips. Dear God, had it been as long ago as Saturday night since he'd kissed those lips? How had he managed to be with her for almost three hours now and not kiss her senseless?

"I want you."

He spoke his thoughts honestly and without any consideration of her reaction.

Jamie's gaze seemed welded with his. Her mouth dropped open, and her eyes widened in surprise. "You...what?"

Neither seemed aware that Chris was blowing bubbles in his Coke.

Mitch leaned across the table and said in a husky, no-nonsense voice, "I want to take Chris home, put him to bed and then put you to bed. My bed."

"B-but you said you only wanted one night."

He sensed her indecision and realized that she'd had no idea what he expected from her after Saturday night. He urged a half smile to his lips in an effort to allay her fears. "I lied. Guys do that, you know, to get women to do what they want."

Jamie heard the teasing quality in his voice. She tried to ignore her heart, which pounded in anticipation of another night in his arms. The worry in her eyes softened as she replied, "I suspected as much."

"And you don't mind?"

"No," she said, with a shake of her head, "I don't mind at all."

Two hours later Mitch pulled Jamie's sweater off. "You're so beautiful."

Jamie smiled her thanks and did the same for him, running her fingers through the crisp hair adorning his chest. "I love the hair on your chest."

"I'll grow more," he quipped, tossing her skirt on top of the slacks she'd taken off him seconds before.

"That has to be ironed!"

"I'll get Mrs. Henley to do it in the morning."

Jamie gasped. "I can't stay all night!"

"You'll be too tired to drive home," he promised.

"What will she think?"

"That we've made love, probably. Will you step out of those damned panty hose, Jamie?" She did as he said and smiled when he groaned. "What are you trying to do? Give me cardiac arrest?"

"What do you mean?" she asked, knowing good and well what he meant.

"You aren't wearing any underwear!"

"I was wearing panty hose, Mitch," she explained, batting her eyelashes at him.

He mumbled something she couldn't hear and peeled off his socks. Jamie's ecru bra was unclasped and tossed upward, where it landed on a blade of the ceiling fan, to hang there like a forgotten party streamer.

Smiling, Mitch rubbed his palms together the way Chris did when he saw something he wanted. Then he pulled her naked body against him and kissed her.

The teasing atmosphere fled the room. Her mouth parted; his mouth possessed. They kissed...hungry, bruising kisses that fueled a desire already blazing out of control. For endlessly long moments the only sounds in the room were sighs and moans, whispered praise and murmured promises, the rustling of flesh against crisp percale sheets and, finally, simultaneous cries of uninhibited passion as Mitch and Jamie reached the edge of the world and tumbled off the other side—not into darkness as many through the years predicted, but into a place of glorious, brilliant light.

Later, Jamie lay in Mitch's arms, trying to calm the beating of her heart and regulate the harshness of her breathing.

"I told you it would work well, didn't I?" Mitch said, recalling the statement he'd made to her that seemed so long ago.

She nodded. "You were right. It does work. Very, very well."

Chapter Twelve

Jamie dropped the manila envelope into the blue mailbox on the corner and breathed a sigh of relief. She'd made the deadline. Her presentation had been typed, her letters of recommendation gathered, her résumé updated and the whole kit and caboodle bundled into a folder and mailed. Now all she had to do was wait and see what happened.

Sam had loved her idea about using the kids as part of a teaching program and seemed to feel that the job was hers; Jamie wasn't so sure. At this point, she really didn't care. She was too caught up with the affair she'd sworn she would never have with Mitch.

It had been a little over a week since that first night, but it seemed to Jamie that they'd been together forever. They had more in common than she ever would have guessed—a love of sports, an interest in art, strong family ties and, of course, their love for Chris.

She put the car in gear and headed toward his house, trying to keep her mind on where they were going that night and not where their relationship was headed. Much to her dismay, they were attending a fund-raiser for one of Mitch's friends who was running for the state senate. She had begged him to go alone, but he had been adamant that she accompany him. The very thought of being thrust into the social strata where she knew she would be as comfortable as a Sunday school teacher at a nudist colony made her stomach churn with apprehension. She expelled a deep breath. The fact that Ian and Karen would be there was her only consolation.

Mitch very carefully refolded the letter from Barstow and slid it into the envelope. He tapped it against his palm, a slight smile toying with his lips. Funny how one's perspective changed with time and circumstance. Now that there was a place for Chris at Barstow, Mitch wasn't sure that was what he wanted to do anymore.

"The…boy…hasss," Chris said, reading from the paper in his lap and stressing the *s* as his speech teacher urged, "the…ball. The…bay-bee…hasss…a rabbutt."

Jamie, who had let herself in by the back door, stood in the doorway of the library with her evening gown draped over her arm, watching and listening as Chris read to Mitch in what was quickly becoming a part of their nightly ritual. It was hard to believe that this was the same Mitchell Bishop she'd met not so long ago. The pride that she had been the catalyst that had prompted him to make some changes in the way he related with Chris was nothing compared to the satisfaction of knowing that the real changes had been made inside Mitch himself.

He was doing more for Chris than ever before. They were going on outings together, and Mitch was supervising Chris's bath, putting him to bed and helping with his homework—whether it was reading, cutting out pictures, teaching him to use the telephone or practicing with money.

He won't need me much longer.

Jamie's heart gave a strange, stumbling lurch as the thought leaped to mind. A bittersweet smile curved her lips. It was something she'd known going into this with Mitch and something she'd chosen to ignore. And since she'd known the possible pitfalls entering their relationship, there was no one to blame but herself. But in one way this time was different, because she intended to enjoy it to the fullest, for however long it lasted.

"How do I look?"

Mitch turned from the mirror, half his face smoothly shaven, the other half covered with thick, creamy lather. His eyes moved over Jamie from the top of her head, where curls were piled in stylish abandon, down to her coral-tipped toes, which peeked from strappy silver sandals. Creamy white shoulders emerged from a strapless gown of jade-green moiré boasting a huge bow that drew attention to the bodice, and a full skirt that enhanced the narrowness of her waist.

Her eyes looked even more vivid against the thicket of her black lashes when paired with the green gown. Skin with the pale translucence he had seen only on models in advertisements managed somehow to make the slight sprinkling of freckles across her nose an attractive embellishment. Coral lipstick lined the fullness of her lips, and the color was repeated by the blush dusting the slight rise of her cheekbones.

"Well," she demanded to know at last, "do I look okay? Or do I look eighteen?"

Mitch heard the anxiety in her voice. "Yes."

"Yes, what?"

"Yes, you look okay. Better than okay. So good, in fact," he told her with a wicked smile, "that I'm seriously considering ripping off all that finery and making love to you instead of going to the shindig."

Her eyes narrowed in feigned anger. "Oh, no you don't. You forced me to agree to this 'shindig,' and now that I'm ready, we're going!"

"Okay. We'll go, but come here a minute." He put down his razor and dried his hands.

Seeing the hunger in his eyes, Jamie took a step backward. "Mitch..."

"Come here, Jamie," he said, loosening the royal-blue towel at his hips.

He was so beautiful, she thought as the towel fell to the floor and her eyes roamed him hungrily, charting the flat planes of his abdomen and the trickling of hair down his stomach. Except for the thick white scars around his knee, there wasn't a thing to mar his masculine beauty. With a sigh because she couldn't help herself, Jamie did as he commanded.

When she reached him, Mitch gathered two fistfuls of her gown and began to pull it up.

Her eyes widened in shock. She hadn't really thought he would... "Mitch! You can't do this."

"Wanna bet?" he asked, backing her against the double vanity.

Memory of the last bet she'd made with him rose in her mind. She sighed. "No. I don't want to bet. But," she warned as he bunched the fabric up around her waist and draped the bulk of it behind her across the marble top of the vanity, "if you wrinkle this dress..."

Mitch's mouth puckered and aimed a playful kiss in her direction. Jamie ducked instinctively from the touch of his lips, as much to avoid the shaving cream as to keep from ruining her lipstick.

"...or ruin my makeup..."

His hands were at the waistband of her panty hose. He inched the sheerness over her hips. "Mitch Bishop, if you ruin these hose, I'll..."

Her voice trailed away, her eyes closed, and her teeth sank into her bottom lip as his hand skimmed the tight curls at the juncture of her thighs and his fingers slipped into her moist warmth.

"You'll what?" he queried.

Her eyes opened. They were filled with an unlikely combination of desire and mirth. She was so afraid of losing him. So afraid that what they had was too good to last. "I'll kill you if you stop."

His low, delighted laughter spread throughout the room.

"One more thing," she said.

"Don't wrinkle the dress, don't ruin your makeup, don't ruin your hose...what now?" he asked in a nag-nag-nag voice.

Jamie reached out and touched him, astonished at how he could be so incredibly hard and at the same time so incredibly soft. "Don't let me do this alone."

Mitch's smile was self-deprecating as he said, "Hell, honey, I'm too selfish for that." His hands dragged the panty hose lower and slipped around to cradle the firm flesh of her bottom. Flexing his knees and angling her hips to accommodate him, Mitch thrust into her.

Jamie gave a low groan of pleasure laced with frustration because she couldn't get closer, because he wasn't kissing her, touching her breasts, loving her fully. Her hands gripped the leanness of his hips, her nails carving small crescents in his tanned skin.

"Deeper," she rasped, her breasts swelling against the confines of her gown, aching for his touch.

"I don't want to hurt you."

You'll hurt me when you walk away. "Please."

The look of desperation in her eyes was almost more than he could bear. "Why?"

Because I want you to remember me when you make love to someone else. I want you to remember that I gave you everything I had to give.

"Because I don't ever want another man to come anywhere near making me feel what you do."

Her strange statement made little sense, but Mitch was too far gone to realize it. He moved her and himself slightly in compliance with her demands. "If another man touches you, he's dead," he promised through clenched teeth as his hips found a faster rhythm.

They made love without really touching—a naked, golden-tanned man and an exquisitely frocked woman with her skirts around her bare hips—without any true preliminaries, without so much as a single kiss. He loved her thoroughly. Completely. Deeply.

When it was over and their breathing had returned to normal and her dishabille had been repaired—and while Jamie's slender finger etched a heart in the shaving cream still on his face—Mitch said quietly, "Marry me."

The two simple words bounced off the tiled walls and echoed through her heart. Was this really happening? Was she really standing in the middle of Mitch's bathroom in an expensive evening gown while he—stark naked—proposed marriage to her?

"Why?"

Mitch, who was tucking the discarded towel around his waist, looked up in surprise. "Why?" he repeated. "Isn't that obvious?"

Tell me you love me. Me. Not what I do. Not because I know how to handle Chris. Me.

She shrugged. "It would be nice to hear."

"All right, then. Chris and I need you."

As soon as the words left his mouth and he saw the look on Jamie's face, Mitch wanted to snatch them back. Even though he'd meant them in more ways than he even realized, he knew they were the wrong words, given knowledge of her past. He cursed himself for a fool and searched for the right words to rectify the situation.

Reaching out, he lifted her chin and forced her to meet his eyes. "I'm not your ex-husband, Jamie."

"I know."

"What we have is good, and I don't want to lose it."

Her eyes filled, and one teardrop trickled down her cheek. "Neither do I."

"Good." He smiled and feathered a kiss to her temple. His thumb brushed the moisture from her cheek. "No tears. You'll ruin your makeup."

Her reciprocal smile was a miserable failure.

"I know this came as a surprise. And I know we haven't known each other very long. I won't rush you. You can have all the time you need to decide."

"It will never work, Mitch," she said.

"Wanna bet?" he asked with a smile.

She shook her head, and this time her smile was genuine but weak. "No."

"Afraid you'll lose again?" he taunted, pulling her close.

Jamie shook her head and leaned against him. She didn't have the heart to tell him that she didn't want to bet because she was too much of a coward to even try to make it work.

Jamie stood beside Mitch, who looked devastating in a black tuxedo and pleated shirt, and sipped her champagne in contentment. They had finished the two-hundred-dollar-a-plate dinner, which consisted of an entree of chicken breasts Veronique or crayfish Bordelaise, depending on individual tastes and as a tribute to the state's poultry industry and Cajun influence, respectively.

The mandatory round of after-dinner speeches was over, and the dancing hadn't yet begun. Jamie let the conversation, which dwelt on the upcoming campaign, flow around her while she took the opportunity to soak up the ambience of the marble-floored ballroom, which teemed with campaign hopefuls, their workers and prospective supporters.

Waiters in white jackets moved through the throng, carrying silver trays aloft, keeping glasses filled and empties picked up. The musicians' dais had a veritable forest of greenery as a backdrop for a baby grand piano. Men, looking elegant and dignified in their tuxedos, laughed at jokes, gestured with their drinks, and leaned solicitously toward their partners who, with few exceptions, looked elegant and sophisticated in their designer creations.

Jamie imagined she spotted the styles of Blass, de la Renta, and what looked to her envious but untrained eye like a Carolina Herrera. She was mentally drooling over a particularly fetching black gown when Mitch's voice brought her back to the present with, "Here comes our host, Jamie."

She turned and saw a man who looked like an Irish bear heading toward them, a politician's smile plastered firmly on his florid face. She groaned, a sound that only Mitch could hear, and looked up to see a twinkle of amusement in his brown eyes. "Having fun?"

"I'm awestruck," she said with a small smile.

"Like hell," he told her out of the side of his mouth while he extended his hand and said, "Hello, Larry."

"Mitch!" the rusty-haired man boomed. "How's the sporting goods business?"

The lazy smile that was so attractive lifted the corners of Mitch's mouth. "Can't complain. How's politics?"

"The same as politics has always been."

Mitch laughed and took Jamie's elbow, urging her forward a step. "Larry, I'd like you to meet Jamie Carr, my nephew's teacher. Jamie, this is the party hopeful, Larry Montgomery."

Larry took Jamie's proffered hand in a beefy paw. "Hello, Jamie Carr. What grade do you teach?"

Jamie smiled. There was something likable about the man. "I'm in special education—elementary school."

"A noble occupation," Larry said with an approving nod.

"A needed occupation," she corrected.

"Jamie is totally dedicated and great with those kids," Mitch said.

"Wonderful!"

A flush of pleasure spread through her at Mitch's attention just before she heard a masculine voice ask, "Jamie? Is that you?"

Chad.

Panic exploded inside her at the sound of the voice she'd prayed she'd never have to hear again. She pivoted on one heel to see if there was any possibility that there was something wrong with her hearing and it *wasn't* Chad. From there everything happened in slow-motion horror: her heel slipped on the high-gloss floor. She lost her balance and reached for the nearest thing to steady her, which happened to be Larry Montgomery's arm. In an automatic gesture, he reached out to help her and bumped her arm in the process, and the glass of white wine she was holding showered the front of his shirt, leaving a clear but definitely wet splotch.

She looked up into his face, aghast at what had happened, and tried to ignore the sound of Chad's softly mocking laughter. "I'm sorry."

"No problem," Larry said, his smile securely in place. "I bumped you."

Her throat was thick with unshed tears. "Thank you."

She felt Mitch's hands on her upper arms as he turned her to face him. The look in his eyes asked what was going on, but before she could say anything, Larry held his hand out toward the newcomer and boomed,

"Chad! Glad to see you and Shelly could make it after all!"

Mitch made the connection between the name and Jamie's panic in record speed. The look of understanding on his face and his smile told her everything was going to be all right. He drew her into the curve of his arm while Larry Montgomery urged the interlopers forward. Jamie braced herself for her first look at her former husband in almost six years.

"This is Shelly and Chad Carr of Image Makers," he announced to Mitch and Jamie. "Chad is going to handle my campaign publicity."

Blond and beautiful summed up Chad and Shelly's appearance. Condescension summed up their attitude. The bit of confidence Jamie had gained during the evening evaporated like an early morning mist.

"Shelly, Chad, this is Mitch Bishop—who, if you're a sports fan, needs no further introduction—and his guest, Jamie Carr."

Shelly tucked her hand in Chad's arm and looked up at him, as if giving him permission to handle the potentially volatile situation. Which he did with aplomb and his usual cutting way. He shook hands with Mitch, then faced Jamie with a smug smile on his handsome face.

"Hello, Jamie," he said smoothly. "I see nothing's changed in the last few years."

Jamie's heart sank. She knew exactly what he was talking about, and so would Mitch.

At the look of perplexity on Larry's face, Chad turned the full impact of his considerable charm on the candidate and said, "Jamie and I know each other. Very well, in fact. We used to be married."

Chapter Thirteen

The intrusive ringing of the telephone roused Jamie from a light, fitful sleep. With eyes that rebelled against the sunlight streaming through the spaces of her mini blinds, she groped for the receiver and dragged it to her ear, wondering why she hadn't turned on the answering machine.

"Good morning." Mitch's voice sounded sexy, cheerful and, worst of all, awake. And she knew now that the reason she hadn't turned on the machine was because she didn't want to miss hearing his voice.

"If you say so," she mumbled around a wide yawn.

"Ah, cranky in the mornings, are we?"

A champagne-induced headache tapped lightly at the base of her skull. "*We* aren't, from the sound of your voice, but *I* am."

"What's the matter? Didn't you sleep well?"

"Not very."

"You weren't worried about that little scene with Larry, were you?"

"You didn't spill a glass of wine on the probable next Louisiana state senator."

"Hey, honey, ease up. Larry forgot it three minutes after the fact. Are you sure it wasn't seeing your former husband that upset you?"

Jamie was quiet for long seconds. Yes. That was part of the reason she hadn't slept. She had been tormented with memories until the early morning hours. Bittersweet memories of how happy she had been with Chad at first. Bitter memories of the hurtful barbs he'd become so adept at shooting her down with. Sweet memories of Lisa and how much she'd come to love her, only to have to give her up to Shelly.

"Jamie?"

"What?" she asked, too loudly, too sharply.

"You..." He hesitated. "You don't still feel anything for him, do you?"

"No," she said flatly. "Nothing."

"Well, then?"

"It was just hard to see him. I never thought our paths would cross again. After all, they hadn't in all these years. It was simply a nasty shock."

"And you're okay?"

"I'm fine," she assured him. "Or will be once I get a cup of coffee."

"Good. I have a favor to ask."

"Sure. Want me to check your mailbox while you're gone?"

"If you don't mind. It will save Karen a trip every day."

"I don't mind."

"I hate to ask you, but I also need you to keep Chris while I'm gone."

It suddenly felt as if someone had hit Jamie in the stomach with a two-by-four. History did repeat itself, she thought.

"Jamie? Are you going back to sleep?"

"No! No. I'm fine. Where's Mrs. Henley?"

"She had to leave for Spokane early this morning. The nursing home called and said her mother was really bad."

"I see."

Mitch heard the hesitation in her voice. "Look, if it's a problem, I can—"

"No. It's no problem. Really."

"Yes, it is. Any kid would be. You don't know how much I appreciate it."

I love you Mitch. Jamie's eyes closed, and a single tear slid down her cheek. "I know."

"I'll pack a suitcase for him to bring to school, and I'll leave the key in the pot of pansies on the back porch so you can pick up extra clothes for him if you need to."

"Okay." Her voice sounded dull and lifeless even to herself.

"Jamie?"

"What?" she asked, blinking back the threatening tears.

"Think about what I asked you while I'm gone. Will you?"

Was that insecurity she heard in his voice? "Yes," she whispered.

"Promise?"

"Yes. How long will you be gone?"

"I'll be in really late Friday night, so I'll probably wait to pick Chris up on Saturday morning, if that's okay."

"That's fine."

"How about breakfast?"

"That sounds like a good idea," she said with a nod as she brushed the tears from her face.

"Are you catching cold?"

"Allergies," she lied. "It's the season."

There was a long pause, and then he said, "I miss you already."

The softly spoken words made Jamie begin to cry in earnest. She cried because she didn't know what to do. She cried for her inability to discern the truth from her wishful thinking...or from the scars of insecurity left behind by Chad and Paul.

Thankfully, Mitch thought she was crying because he was leaving.

"You're kidding!" Leah said that afternoon as she sat munching on a granola bar during the free period she shared with Jamie. "Your ex was at the fundraiser?"

Jamie nodded.

"And..." Leah asked, gesturing for more information.

"And when I heard him say my name, I lost my balance, fell into Larry Montgomery's arms and spilled my wine all over his shirt in the process."

Leah couldn't help the hoot of laughter that escaped her. When Jamie only looked more forlorn, she did her best to control her mirth. "I'm sorry, Jamie, but, honestly!"

"I could have crawled into a hole. Larry was very nice about it, and at least it wasn't red wine, but damn! Why then? Why in front of Chad?"

"What did Mitch say?"

"He told me not to worry about it. He laughed and said I'd made a lasting impression on Larry and that it was no big deal. But, Leah! He's running for the senate!"

Leah shrugged, clearly unimpressed with Larry Montgomery's credentials. "What did good old Chad have to say when he found out you were there with Mitch Bishop?"

"Nothing, really, but I could tell he couldn't believe it. After all, dates with former superstars and political gatherings are not my usual style."

"They are now," Leah reminded her.

Jamie didn't answer that. She only sat there staring out the window at the children romping in the spring sunshine.

Seeing the misery on her friend's face, Leah asked, "Are you sorry?"

"That I went to the fund-raiser?"

"No, goose. That you decided to...to..." She paused, searching for the right word.

"To have an affair with Mitch?" Jamie said bluntly. "No. Yes. Sometimes."

"I always did like a straight answer," Leah quipped.

Offering her a wan smile, Jamie said, "He wants to marry me."

"He wants to... Jamie, that's wonderful! It's..." Her voice trailed away when she failed to see any enthusiasm in Jamie's eyes. "You did tell him yes, didn't you?"

"I haven't told him anything yet. He told me to take my time."

Leah looked disbelieving. "Good grief, what's holding you back? Surely not this silly paranoia you have about being clumsy."

"No. As embarrassing as that is, it's hardly reason to turn down a marriage proposal, especially when you're knocking on the door of the big three-o," Jamie said with a semblance of her usual spunk.

"Then what?" Leah pressed. As if a sudden thought struck her, she said, "Oh. Is it the money thing? The difference in your life-styles?"

"Partly."

"That's ridiculous! If you love someone enough, all that can be worked out."

"Maybe so. But there's Chris."

"Oh, Jamie! Surely you can't think . . . ?"

"Why not?" she asked with perfect logic. "Two others put it over on me. Why not Mitch?"

"Because he's . . ."

"Because he's Mitch Bishop, former football hero and business magnate?"

"Don't you think that's unfair?"

"Is it?" Jamie shot back. "Then you tell me why he called this morning and asked if Chris could stay at my house this week while he makes another trip to Chicago."

"I thought he had a baby-sitter hired."

"He does. She's going to see her sick mother in Spokane."

"Well, that explains it, then, doesn't it?"

Jamie rose from her desk and began to pace the room. "Who knows?" She heaved a sigh of disgust. "Why didn't he get someone else? Why call me when he's made it a point to let me know he can afford the best care for Chris?"

Leah shook her head. "I can't answer that, except for the obvious: he trusts you. What did you tell him?"

"I told him yes, of course."

There was a hint of a smile on Leah's face. "I like the way you stand up for what you think is right."

"Yeah. Sure. I'm a fool, right?"

Leah crossed the room and tossed her wrapper into the wastebasket. Then she gave Jamie a brief hug and said, "No. Not a fool. Just a person with a huge capacity for love."

"And where did it ever get me?"

There was sincerity in the blue eyes that bored into Jamie's. "Didn't you ever read that you reap what you sow?"

Jamie nodded, frowning.

"If that's true, Jamie, you're in for a bountiful harvest."

"No you! Mitz!"

Chris was adamant about Jamie's not overseeing his bath that first night. Only when Mitch called and persuaded him via the phone did the child relent and get into the tub for Jamie.

It was the same every night. He wanted Mitch. He wanted his bedroom. He wanted his house. He didn't want Jamie doing anything for him. He wouldn't read for her, wouldn't mind, wouldn't eat. Besides exhibiting the stubbornness she was used to dealing with on a smaller scale, Chris was also depressed.

At first Jamie wondered if he thought Mitch had gone away as his parents had, but when she began to realize he waited beside the phone for Mitch's call, she decided that wasn't the case. Very simply, Chris missed his uncle.

So did Jamie.

But missing him and wanting him didn't change the fears that haunted her. Should she accept his proposal of marriage and take a chance that it might work? Was she a fool if she did?

By the time Mitch arrived to pick Chris up on Saturday morning, she was a wreck, but she had made her decision.

She loved Mitch. More than she had ever loved Chad. More than she could ever imagine loving anyone. But her scars and insecurities about herself and her fear of Mitch's real motivation for asking her were too deeply ingrained. Besides, he had never said he loved her, and though his lovemaking was good, right, wonderful, it wasn't love.

"Chris and I need you."

But they didn't, as this week had shown her. Mitch was all Chris needed now, and Mitch didn't need her to help him with their communication anymore. The truth was that she wasn't strong enough to wait for him to tell her he didn't need her anymore. It was better to give him up now than later, when she'd learned to love him even more.

The first thing Mitch noticed when she let him in on Saturday morning was that she had lost some weight. The second thing he saw were the dark circles smudged beneath her eyes. After saying his hellos to a jubilant Chris, he pulled Jamie into his arms and rocked her from side to side. "Rough week, Teach?"

Jamie clung to him and nodded against his shoulder.

"Miss me?"

"Yes."

He sighed in satisfaction. "Did you think about us?" he asked, pushing aside her shirt and kissing her bare shoulder.

"Yes."

"And?" He cast a look at Chris, who was engrossed in Saturday morning cartoons, and unbuttoned the top two buttons of her shirt.

Jamie pulled back to look at him, capturing his hands before they began to wreak havoc on her shaky resolve. "I . . . I need more time."

A shaft of pain pierced Mitch's heart. If she really loved him, wouldn't she say yes? Would she need so much time?

"Okay," he told her, doing up the buttons again and telling himself not to worry. "You've got it. How about dinner tonight? I can get Karen to baby-sit."

"I can't."

"I know you're tired, but I'll get you home early."

"I'm sorry. I can't have breakfast, either. I'm leaving for Arkansas in a few minutes," she told him, unable to meet the directness of his gaze.

Panic gripped him. She hadn't mentioned taking a trip before. "Your folks live there, don't they?"

"Yes. Camden."

Don't push, Bishop. Give her some room. She's been alone for a long time. She just needs to think things through.

"Well," he said with a heartiness he was far from feeling, "it'll be good for you to visit them. Especially after the week you've had."

"Yeah. It will be." She did meet his eyes then, and the forced gaiety in her voice didn't mesh with what he saw there.

"I'd better go so you can get on the road. It's a long drive. Be careful."

"I will."

Mitch leaned forward and kissed her, then grabbed Chris's suitcase. Chris gave her a goodbye hug, and she watched them drive away, the hot tears scalding her eyes and sliding down her cheeks. Mitch didn't know it, but he was driving out of her life. But he would never be out of her heart.

Arkansas was the same as always. Her mother was still busy with her bridge club; her father was planting his vegetable garden. They both knew something was wrong but wisely kept their own counsel until she decided to tell them. But when her brother, Michael—buyer of the strange house slippers—asked about her love life, Jamie burst into tears.

In the end, the telling was cathartic, but she still had no solutions to her dilemma. Dreading the long drive back to Baton Rouge and asking herself why she hadn't flown into Little Rock and driven on to Camden, Jamie called Sam on Sunday and told him she wouldn't be in to teach on Monday. He assured her there was no problem, and she left her parents' house after breakfast and pulled into her apartment complex at six o'clock on Monday evening, thoroughly tired and miserable.

As she was carrying in her suitcase, the phone began to ring. Afraid it would be Mitch but knowing she had to face him sooner or later, she picked up the re-

ceiver, interrupting the answering machine's programmed hello.

"Hello."

"Jamie!" a masculine voice boomed. "This is Sam.
How was the trip?"

She couldn't help the weary smile that pulled at her
lips when she heard the enthusiasm in his voice. "Tiring. Remind me never to drive up there when I can afford to fly."

"Done," Sam said with a laugh.

"What's up? Did the substitute teacher jump out
the window?"

Sam laughed again, since the jump was all of three
feet. "No. I just thought I'd let you know that Gayle
called me today to let me know you got the job. The
school board will be calling you in for an interview in
a few days, but it's only a formality. You are now the
parish supervisor of special education."

Jamie absorbed his news with little reaction. Where
was the happiness she should be feeling? The joy for
a job well done?

"Hey! Where's the old enthusiasm?" Sam asked,
almost echoing her thoughts.

"I guess I'm just tired. It's been a hectic three-day
weekend—on top of having Chris for a week."

"Yeah. I can relate. Well, kiddo, I'll let you get
back to whatever you were doing, and I'll see you tomorrow."

"Thanks for calling, Sam."

"Sure. Congratulations."

"Thanks. 'Bye."

She cradled the phone and sat staring at it, wondering if she would ever feel anything that resembled
happiness again.

She was still unpacking twenty minutes later when the doorbell rang. With her heart beating ninety to nothing she went downstairs and unlocked the door.

Mitch stood there, appearing as haggard and miserable as she felt. He looked as if he hadn't shaved since she left, and his eyes were as shadowed as hers. His hair had been ravaged by nervous fingers.

"Where in the hell have you been?" he asked, torn between the urge to pull her into his arms and kiss her or to shake her senseless. Doing neither, he stepped inside at Jamie's tacit invitation.

Jamie's heart sank, weighed down by the fact that just because the decision was made didn't make it any easier to live with.

"I decided to stay an extra day."

"Why didn't you call and let me know?"

Jamie urged a false smile forward. "I didn't know I was supposed to check in. Sorry," she told him with brittle lightness.

The disbelief on Mitch's face could have won a prize. Hands on his hips, he looked at her, trying to figure out what was going on. "I was worried about you," he said at last. I didn't know how to find out if you were all right or not. I finally called Sam this afternoon, and he told me you were supposed to be in this evening."

Jamie pushed aside the possibility that he was genuinely worried about her. "I'm sorry. I just never thought to call," she lied.

He stared at the floor. "What happened?" he asked at last, raising his head and looking at her with bleak brown eyes.

"What do you mean?"

"I mean what happened while you were in Arkansas to make you like this?"

"Like what?" she asked innocently.

"Like you could care less that I was worried about you. Like you could care less if you never saw me again. Like what we shared together never happened."

It took every ounce of strength Jamie possessed to face him without letting the tears stinging behind her eyelids fall. "That isn't true," she whispered, realizing with a start that she couldn't go through with it. She wasn't strong enough to take his leaving her or tiring of her, but she wasn't strong enough to end it, either.

Wringing her hands, she tried to think of something to say that would fix what she'd done. How could she repair the rift between them? Finally, because the silence stretching between them seemed to border on forever, she said the first thing that came to mind.

"Did Sam tell you the news?"

Mitch, who was staring at a spot across the room, shook his head, but it was obvious his mind wasn't on her question.

"I got the job."

His gaze flew to hers, his eyes bright and hard. "You got the job?" His worry over the past twenty-four hours, his continued anguish over her failure to respond to his proposal and her inexplicable coolness at seeing him again were all beginning to coalesce into a dangerous brew of fractured emotions. What he'd most feared was coming to pass: he'd given Jamie his heart, and she was walking away from it. Irrational anger was rearing its head to guard him from the hurt he knew was forthcoming.

"Yes," she said, offering him a tentative smile. "I want to thank you. I probably wouldn't have gone through with it if you hadn't pushed."

Mitch began to laugh, soft laughter that was somehow frightening. "I'm beginning to understand."

"Understand what?"

He pinned her with a relentless stare. "What's the matter with you. It's all perfectly clear now."

"What's perfectly clear?"

He said the one thing that made the most sense amid the maelstrom of emotions punishing him. "The reason you were so wishy-washy about our relationship. You were just waiting to see if you got the damned job! And now that you have it, it's obviously over between us. Pardon me for being so slow on the uptake." He raked his hand through his hair and turned to go.

Jamie couldn't believe what was happening. "What do you mean?" she asked, reaching out and grabbing his arm. "Where are you going?"

He looked pointedly at the hand on his arm. "Somewhere away from here." He lifted his gaze to hers. "I thought I saw something different in you, but I was wrong. The packaging is different, that's all. You look like the kind of woman who wants to share her life with people, not pursue power. But inside you're no different from all the other women scaling the corporate ladder."

Jamie stared at him, unable to believe what she was hearing. None of this made any sense!

He pried her fingers from his arm and let her hand fall to her side. "I admire your determination to get ahead. Really. And I understand how marriage to me and caring for Chris can't hold a candle to your rising career in education!''

He went to the door and opened it, and Jamie was powerless to think of a way to stop him. He was out the door and had started to close it when he stuck his head back in and added with caustic sarcasm, ''By the way, Larry is single. Play your cards right, and he might get you a spot on the school board.''

After he left, Jamie cried, called herself a fool and cried some more. It wasn't easy to think when all she could visualize was Mitch walking out her door. For some reason she couldn't fathom, he believed that her new job was behind her not calling him and her cool, negative behavior when he got there. She told herself it was for the best; it was what she'd wanted to do but hadn't had the guts for. But it still hurt. Terribly.

She didn't sleep all night, and when the alarm began beeping at six, she shut it off and headed for the shower, thankful that the long night was over. Even after a hot shower and several cups of coffee, Jamie wondered how she would make it through the day.

She had barely stowed her purse in her bottom desk drawer when Sam's voice came over the loudspeaker, asking her to come to his office. Jamie went with a feeling of foreboding. Was there any good that could come when she was feeling so low?

Sam handed her a cup of coffee the minute she stepped through the door. Then he settled himself on the edge of his desk. ''Mitch has taken Chris out of school and is putting him in Barstow. Effective today,'' he said bluntly.

The Styrofoam cup of coffee slipped from Jamie's nerveless fingers onto her lap, and she leaped to her feet with a cry of distress. Sam was beside her in an instant, thrusting a wad of paper toweling at her. Jamie blotted up the spill as best she could, while Sam stood looking out the window, his hands jammed into his pockets.

"What's going on, Jamie?" he asked, turning to face her.

The tender solicitation broke down all her reserves. She didn't answer. The tears that had never been far from the surface since Mitch walked out her door filled her eyes and raced down her cheeks. Swearing softly, Sam reached for the intercom asking his secretary to have his wife come to the office.

Leah arrived in a matter of moments. She took one look at Jamie and gave her a motherly hug, smoothing Jamie's tousled hair with a caring hand. "Tell me," she said.

And Jamie did, letting out her fears, her grief and her tears in a flood that seemed never ending.

"It sounds to me as if Mitch is guilty of the same thing you are," Sam said when she had mopped up most of her tears.

Jamie sniffed and blew her nose. "What's that?"

"Jumping to wrong conclusions," Leah said, knowing instantly what Sam was getting at. "Just because of your past, you lumped him in the same category with the other men you've known, and that wasn't fair to either you or Mitch."

"And how did he do the same thing?" Jamie asked, failing to see the connection.

"The first day I met Mitch, when we were barbecuing at your place, he said you were different from the kind of woman he dealt with, because you weren't clawing your way to the top or interested only in money or success," Sam confided. "Maybe now, with all the other worries he's got, he thinks you *are* like all those women, especially since you told him about the job at a time when he knew there was something wrong between you."

Jamie sighed. Right or wrong, it made a bit of sense. "And he put Chris in Barstow to get back at me?"

Sam winced. "Ouch. Give him a little credit. I imagine he did it because leaving him here would be too much of a reminder of you."

"You're right. There could be any number of reasons," she said with a sigh. "I guess I'm just not thinking straight."

"You're not thinking at all," Sam said. "I suspect neither of you is." He put his hand on her shoulder and propelled her gently toward the door. "I'll call the substitute back for the day. You go on home and try to get some rest. Maybe things will look better tomorrow."

Jamie offered Sam a tired smile. "Thanks, Sam." She gave him and Leah a hug and left the room.

Forty minutes later, she was at home in her bed, sound asleep.

Chapter Fourteen

Jamie's heartache and exhaustion were so deep that she didn't wake up until almost four-thirty that afternoon. She didn't hurt as much, but that was probably because she wasn't awake yet. She was a little hungry but couldn't find enough energy to get up and fix something to eat.

It's all your fault. If you'd only had more confidence in yourself, if you'd loved him enough to trust him...

He never said he loved you, her mind argued.

Impulsively, Jamie reached for the phone and dialed Mitch's number. His answering machine came on after the third ring. "Hi. I'm away from the phone right now..." The rest of his message was lost in the maelstrom of emotions that hit her at the sound of his voice.

Oh, Mitch, what have I let happen? She replaced the receiver and fell back against the bed, flinging her arm across her closed eyes in an effort to block out the world.

Moments later, after telling herself she had to become part of the world again, she rewound her own cassette to listen to the messages she'd received while she was in Arkansas. She heard the sound of her recorded message, and then, surprisingly, Mitch's voice filled the room.

"Hi. I know this is silly, since you won't hear this until you get back and you haven't been gone even an hour, but I wanted to call you and let you know how much I miss you." She pressed her knuckles against her lips, and her eyes brimmed with more of the hated tears. "It's been so long since I've really talked to you or kissed you."

He paused, and she heard a sigh come through the phone lines. "Jamie, Jamie, I've never wanted anyone like I want you. I just wanted you to know that. Good night, honey. Sweet dreams."

Jamie closed her eyes and put her hands over her ears to shut out the sound of his voice, which still echoed inside her head, but the recordings followed one another just like night follows day, one for every day she'd been gone. And nothing and no one on the face of God's green earth could have stopped her from listening.

"Good morning, honey. Did you sleep well? I didn't. I kept waking up and thinking that you should be here beside me." He laughed. "I even thought I could smell your shampoo on my pillow. Did I ever tell you that your shampoo smells like summer sunshine? And your eyes... Ah, Jamie, I could drown in those green eyes of yours. Uh-oh. Chris is calling, so I gotta go. By the way, he dialed your number for me all by himself. He's really getting good. We miss you. Hurry and get home, Teach, okay?''

Jamie turned the machine off, unable to listen to any more for the harsh sobs that shook her.

Later that evening she decided she could listen without crying.

She was wrong.

She was playing his Monday morning message while she picked at a frozen dinner. Her shoulders slumped when she heard how tired and dejected he sounded.

''Where are you, Jamie? Why didn't you come home last night, and why haven't you called? I worry that you might have had an accident, and no one would even let me know. I'm going crazy, and so is Chris. He really misses you. All he keeps talking about is Hay-mee's house. I don't know what you've done to us, lady, but you have two admirers forever. Oh, Jamie, I love you so much I hurt inside.''

''I love you so much I hurt inside.'' Why hadn't he ever told her before? Why... Her hand came up over her mouth to stifle a keening wail while the machine played relentlessly on.

''I want to share the rest of my life with you. I know it will be hard with Chris, but... Oh, hell, a telephone message isn't the place for all this, is it? I miss you, honey. Please come home this evening.''

The machine clicked off, and Jamie sat staring at it, knowing without a doubt that she'd blown her chance for happiness and not certain she could ever find it again. If she tried to go to Mitch, would he even listen?

We're adults. Of course he'd listen.

Then why didn't you talk to him like an adult and tell him your fears?

He might have lied about his feelings.

Not Mitch.

"Not Mitch," she repeated aloud. "Not Mitch."

Call him.

He might not understand.

How will you know if you don't call?

I'm afraid. I can't.

But in the end, she did call before she left for school the next morning. All she got was his machine. And the sound of his voice only made her more aware of what she'd lost.

Mitch sat slumped in a chair, staring through the room's darkness, a glass of liquid forgetfulness in his hand, his heart heavy with the burden of his double loss. How had it come to this? How had he let it all slip through his fingers? How had he misjudged her so badly?

Love is blind. Joyce's voice from the past taunted him with remembrances.

You're right, Joyce. It is.

Mitz! Mitz!

Mitch bolted upright, his ear turned toward Chris's bedroom and the unmistakable sound of Chris crying out his name. Then he remembered, and his body sagged against the chair's back. Chris wasn't upstairs anymore. Chris was in Barstow, at least for now.

It had been a stupid, immature move to take him from the school he was used to. But it had seemed the only possible thing to do in the face of the heartache Jamie had thrust upon him. Karen and Ian had quietly accepted his decision. Quite simply and selfishly, he hadn't thought of Chris. He'd thought only of severing all connection with Jamie.

He was leaving for a short trip to Dallas early the next morning, but when he got back, he would reconsider sending Chris to public school so he could be at home at night. He hadn't been gone twenty-four hours yet, and already the big house echoed with memories of Chris's voice—his laughter, his serious tones as he read, his adamant, stubborn "No!"

Downing the last of the potent liquor, he pushed himself unsteadily to his feet. He made it to his room, where he toppled onto the masculine comforter and fell instantly into a dreamless, Chivas Regal sleep.

Somehow Jamie made it through Wednesday and Thursday. She wasn't better by any means, but she'd learned that the body and mind possessed miraculous checks and balances. You could only cry so many tears, only hurt as badly as she had for so long. And then your body shut down—at least hers had—and a blessed numbness took over. And, as it had been before, work became her cure-all.

She took the kids outside for a nature excursion, they drew spring flowers, they became acquainted with their new mascot, Jerome, a ferret that one of the fathers had donated to replace Lester. And through it all, she wondered how Mitch and Chris were faring. Was Mitch hurting as much as she was? Did Chris, in spite of her worries, like Barstow?

The nights were the worst times. Once she had prepared her lesson materials for the next day, there was nothing to do but stare at television programs she didn't really see and listen to Mitch's recordings over and over again.

She entered the apartment on Friday afternoon and dumped her books on the sofa, mentally preparing herself for the longed-for weekend. Thank goodness she wouldn't have to put forth any effort to act as if everything were okay. She'd work in her flower beds, she thought as she rewound the cassette on the answering machine, then set it to play back.

"Hello. This is Jamie. I can't come to the phone..." She let the message play against the backdrop of her mind, trying to focus on dinner. She unbuttoned her aqua-and-white-striped blouse and tugged it from the waistband of the matching aqua skirt with one hand, while the other shuffled through the cans on the upper shelf of the cabinet.

Canned Chinese. Asparagus.

"Ms. Carr. This is Sylvie at the bookstore. We got in that Stephen King book you ordered. You can pick it up whenever you like. See you soon."

Good, she thought with a smile, moving aside a jar of Ragu and uncovering a can of mixed bean salad.

"Hay-mee!"

Jamie's head snapped toward the answering machine. "Chris?" she said incredulously, nearing the phone with a feeling of awed disbelief. She turned up the volume, and Chris's tear-laden voice, raised in anguish and terror, continued to ramble incoherently. "Mitz! Mitz house. Hay-mee house. No 'cool. Go Hay-mee 'cool. Chris go Hay-mee—"

The words were shut off abruptly as the phone he was using was recradled. How had he gotten to a phone? she wondered. And more importantly, what should she do?

Mitch, she thought, reaching for the phone. She had called several times, hoping she could talk to him and try to work things out, but she got his answering machine every time, and he'd never returned her calls.

She got the picture. He wasn't interested in hearing what she had to say, so she'd vowed she wouldn't call again. But this was different. She had to call and let him know how unhappy Chris was. Her hand paused in midair. But surely Mitch was in contact with the personnel at Barstow. Surely they had told him whether Chris was settling in or not. And surely, if Mitch knew he was unhappy, he wouldn't force him to stay. Jamie grabbed the receiver. Whatever the situation, she intended to let him know Chris's immediate condition.

She dialed Mitch's number and almost gnashed her teeth in frustration when she got his answering machine again. Didn't the man ever stay home and answer his phone? She chewed on her bottom lip and twisted a lock of her hair, wondering what to do next.

The plant! To save time she got the number from local information and punched it in.

"Bishop's Sporting Goods," said a pleasant-voiced woman.

"Is Mr. Bishop in, please?"

"I'm sorry, ma'am, but Mr. Bishop is out of town and won't be returning until late tonight. Would you like to leave a message?"

"No. No thank you." Jamie hung up the receiver and stared at the telephone. Now what? Whom should she call? The sound of Chris's sobbing voice played through her mind. "I'm trying, Chris. I'm trying," she said aloud.

On impulse, she got Barstow's number and called it.

"Barstow." The answering voice was cool and professional, which translated unfairly in Jamie's mind as unflappable and uncaring.

"Hello," she said, unable to prevent the coolness in her own voice. "My name is Jamie Carr, and I'm a friend of Mitchell Bishop's."

At the mention of Mitch's name the faceless voice perked up considerably. "Oh? What can I do for you?"

"Well, actually, I'm calling to see how his nephew, Chris Decker, is settling in."

"Oh, Chris is doing very well. No problems."

Jamie knew she was about to overreact—after all, she was probably talking to a receptionist—but she didn't care.

"Then maybe you can tell me why there was a hysterical message from him on my answering machine when I got in this afternoon?" No doubt about it, that was out-and-out accusation she heard in her own voice.

For several seconds there was complete silence on the other end of the line. When the woman spoke again, the temporary friendliness was buried beneath an avalanche of coldness. "If Chris was crying, Ms. Carr, it was probably because he was reprimanded for unauthorized tampering with the phones."

"He was crying, almost incoherent, *before* anyone knew he was on the phone."

"Are you insinuating—"

"I'm not insinuating anything," Jamie told her calmly. "I simply feel that he's naturally upset because he's in a strange place and obviously missing his uncle. If that's all that's wrong, then you have no reason to be on the defensive, do you?'' Her implication was very clear.

"You're right, of course," the woman said. "I merely felt you were attacking Barstow, and our reputation has always been above reproach."

Jamie grimaced. "Yes. I know. May I talk to Chris?"

"I'm sorry, but he's in bed."

"At five o'clock in the afternoon?"

"Yes, well, he's been outside most of the day. He was tired."

"I see," Jamie said, suddenly seeing very well. "Maybe tomorrow, then."

"Of course. Tomorrow." The unknown woman's voice was jovial now.

"Well, goodbye, then," Jamie said as pleasantly as possible. "Thank you for your time."

She hung up and sank back against the sofa cushions. While it was possible that the woman was telling the truth, Jamie had a different idea about why Chris was sleeping. If he was being typically Chris—acting the way he had acted with her, or worse—he was a handful. He must have wandered away from whoever was supervising him at some point in the day and called her.

He'd been discovered, obviously. And then what? Had they sedated him? Was that why he was asleep at this time of day? While mild sedation was a perfectly valid thing to do in cases of extreme excitability or destructive behavior, it broke Jamie's heart to think they'd had to use such measures on Chris. If Chris was behaving badly, it was only because he was miserable, out of his element. And if that were the case, something had to be done. Now. Tonight.

She called Ian and Karen Forrest's number as quickly as information could give it to her.

"Hello?"

"Karen? This is Jamie Carr."

"Jamie! What a nice surprise! I was afraid I'd never hear from you again now that you and Mitch..." Her voice trailed away as she realized she'd stuck her foot in her mouth. "Oops! I shouldn't have brought it up. I'm sorry."

"It's all right." Anxious to steer the conversation away from her and Mitch, Jamie said, "Do you and Ian have any legal say over what happens to Chris while Mitch is out of town?"

Karen's voice clearly asked what was going on as she said, "As a matter of fact, Ian and I made the drive to Barstow with Mitch and Chris. All three of us signed the admissions form and custody papers. Is anything wrong?"

Jamie told her what had happened during the last few minutes.

"Oh, poor little Chris!" Karen cooed. "Look, Ian should be here any minute, and as soon as he gets here, we'll meet you and go on out there. We'll worry about what Mitch says when he gets here."

Jamie sighed in relief. "Thanks, Karen. I'll be waiting."

One hour and ten minutes later, Jamie, Ian and Karen marched up the wide, curving flagstone steps of Barstow. A huge open area filled with greenery and enough priceless art to qualify the school as a museum served as a reception room. A middle-aged woman sat behind a Queen Anne desk.

Ian glanced over at Jamie. "Karen and I will handle this," he told her with an encouraging smile.

Jamie nodded. After all, she had no authority to do anything about Chris's condition.

The woman looked up as the trio approached.

Ian sauntered to the desk with that graceful gait of his. "Hullo, luv," he said pleasantly, tossing down several pieces of identification. "I'm Ian Forrest, Chris Decker's uncle. My wife and I would like to check Chris out for a few days."

The woman's eyes darted over Ian's credentials, glanced up into his handsome face and flickered over his companions. "I'm afraid that's impossible at this hour, Mr. Forrest."

Jamie recognized the woman's voice from their earlier telephone conversation.

Ian sat down on the edge of the desk supported by delicate cabriole legs and said, "Really, luv? Why is that?"

The woman, whose name plate read, *MRS. GRIFFEN*, blushed, evidently willing to overlook Ian's crassness in face of his considerable charm. "Well, we have rules."

Ian's lips curved upward, giving her the full impact of his smile. "Rules are made to be broken, aren't they? Besides," he tacked on, looking at Karen and giving her a wink that Mrs. Griffen couldn't see, "we've driven a long way out here, and as you can see, my wife is expecting."

Mrs. Griffen was obviously weakening. "If you had called..."

"Is everything all right, Mrs. Griffen?" an austere masculine voice asked. Everyone in the room turned to see a man with a bearing to match Ian's striding toward them.

"Uh, Mr. and Mrs. Forrest would like to check Chris Decker out of the school for a few days."

Ian and the newcomer shook hands over brief introductions.

"And where is Mr. Bishop?"

"My cousin is out of town," Karen piped up. "Tomorrow is my son's birthday, and Chris was expected to be there for the party." Her eyes filled with crocodile tears. "Chris was supposed to spend the weekend, and what will I tell my son? I simply can't believe Mitch forgot to arrange this." She turned pleading blue eyes toward the man. "Can't you make an exception...just this once? I know it's a bother, but other parents have told us time and time again how cooperative you've been."

The unexpected praise evidently tipped the scales in their favor. "Well," the man said as a pleased light entered his pale blue eyes, "I'm sure we can work something out. If you'll just fill out this form..." He snapped his fingers, indicating that Mrs. Griffen should produce the form he needed.

The breath Jamie had been holding whooshed from her in a sigh. Thank goodness. They could get Chris out of here and back with people who loved him. She left Karen and Ian to take care of the paperwork while she went to get Chris and his things together.

He was still sleeping, snoring softly, when she reached his room, and the housemother confessed that she had given him a mild tranquilizer.

Jamie sat on the edge of his bed and shook him with gentle insistence. "Chris, wake up." He moaned and turned onto his side. "C'mon, Chris, wake up. Uncle

Ian and Aunt Karen are here, and we're going to take you home.''

His sleepy-looking eyes opened. For long moments he stared at her while Jamie smiled down at him. Then he returned her smile with a beautiful one of his own and held his arms up. "Hay-mee," he murmured in a groggy voice.

Jamie gathered him close, and Chris hugged her so tightly that she could hardly breathe. But she didn't try to free herself; he needed security, comfort. Finally, as wakefulness penetrated his sleepy mind, he pulled back and looked into her eyes. His mouth turned down in typical Chris fashion. One chubby hand indicated the room in a sweeping gesture. "'Cool, yucky! No me!''

Jamie fought back her tears and offered him a tremulous smile. "You don't have to go to school here anymore, Chris. I promise."

She made the promise, wondering how on earth she would keep it. But at that moment she would have fought an army to keep Chris where he belonged. She would deal with Mitch somehow—for Chris's sake.

By nine o'clock Chris was at home in his own bed. Jamie had persuaded Ian and Karen to leave Chris with her, assuring them she could handle Mitch. Chris wanted to go home instead of her house, and, after a quick journey through Burger King, she had gambled that the key would still be in the pot of pansies. It had been.

Now all she had to do was wait for Mitch to come home and convince him of two things: that both she and Chris needed him.

* * *

Mitch saw the lights in the kitchen and the den from a block away. His first thought was burglars, but burglars would have set off the alarm system. What was going on? he wondered with a combination of fear and irritation spreading through him. It was midnight, and he was past ready for a night of uninterrupted sleep in his own bed. The three days in Dallas had done little to make him forget his misery over what he considered Jamie's deception. And for some reason he couldn't understand, he was worried sick about Chris, even though calls to Barstow had assured him Chris was all right.

All right or not, he was getting Chris out of Barstow the first thing in the morning. What he'd feared from the beginning—that he would learn to love Chris too much—had happened without his being aware that it had.

He turned into the drive, and his headlights slashed through the night, illuminating the front porch, the spring flowers in full bloom and the car sitting in one side of the double garage.

Jamie's car.

Mitch braked to a halt and turned off the key. His heart was beating a mile a minute, and his mouth had gone desert dry. What was Jamie doing here, unless... Chris!

Bolting from the car, he slammed the door and rushed inside, fearing the worst, praying for the best.

She stood in the kitchen, just inside the door, as if she might have been coming to meet him. To Mitch, who was used to reading defense, she looked primed and ready for action. Her chin was high, and so was her color. She wore jeans and a long sweater, and her eyes glittered greenly with that inner fire that drew him so. Her arms were folded across her chest in a manner that suggested she wasn't taking anything from anybody. He noted with thanksgiving that there was nothing in her manner to suggest anything was wrong with Chris.

"I took Chris out of Barstow." She leveled the statement at him in a manner that asked what he intended to do about it. Before he could answer, she rushed on. "He doesn't belong there, Mitch. He called me and got my answering machine. He was crying and calling for you and for me..."

Mitch's eyes closed briefly in pain. *I'm sorry, Chris. I'm so sorry.* He opened his mouth to explain, but she held up her hand in a gesture that warned him not to speak.

"Barstow is probably a wonderful place for kids who were put there as infants or small children who never knew any other life-style. And it's probably a good place for those kids who do become unmanageable. But Chris doesn't fit any of those categories. He isn't unmanageable, and all he's ever known is the love and companionship of a family unit. Chris has his own special place in public school, Mitch. And he's learning so much so fast."

Mitch nodded, thinking how pretty she looked with that fighting look in her eyes.

"It's a crime to make him stay where he's so unhappy."

"I agree."

Jamie was so caught up in her prepared defense that she forged ahead, unaware that Mitch was agreeing with her. "I've promised him he didn't have to go back, and if I have to fight you every inch of the way, I mean to keep that promise."

"I surrender."

She blinked, aware for the first time that he had spoken but not understanding his answer. "What?"

"You're right. Chris isn't going back to Barstow."

"Are you serious?"

He nodded and moved to lean against the cabinets.

"But . . . but why did you take him out of school to begin with?"

"Because . . . I didn't think I could bear to see you anymore," he admitted.

Jamie stared at him, trying to decide how to take that, trying to decide what to say. In the end she decided on honesty, no matter what the result. If the truth wasn't acceptable, they wouldn't be together. And they weren't together now, so what was the difference?

Prompted by the memory of what he'd said on the answering machine—feelings didn't change in a week, did they?—and spurred on by her customary impulsiveness, Jamie moved closer to him.

"I love you, Mitch. I should have told you before. But I was so afraid to trust my feelings—and yours."

The impassive look on Mitch's face faded, and a look of wary interest replaced it.

Her chin angled higher, but her voice was filled with sincerity. "I was wrong to distrust you and your motives because of my past, just the way you were wrong to assume that my job would come between us because of the women you've known."

Mitch was afraid to trust what he was hearing. All he could remember was her inability to make a decision about his proposal and her coolness when she came back from Arkansas.

"When you asked me to marry you, you told me you and Chris needed me, not that you loved me. While I was gone, I decided I'd rather put an end to things now than have you tell me you didn't need me anymore later." She shrugged and gave him a wry smile. "I'm a teacher, but I think I need some lessons in loving and trusting."

A bittersweet smile curved Mitch's mouth. The pain in his heart was erased with one swipe of an unseen hand. "I think we both need that."

A tentative, tremulous smile tugged at the corners of her mouth at his confession, and a ray of hope filled her heart.

He held out his arms, and Jamie went into them without hesitation. He held her, inhaling the breath of sunshine wafting from her hair. Jamie clung to his strength and vowed never to give him a reason to leave.

"I love you, Jamie, and I want you to know that I'll always need you. Always. And not because of Chris. Because of me. Because of you."

He pulled back and kissed her, a tender, love-filled kiss that soothed away the last remnants of her heartache.

"I've missed you, Teach," he said soberly. "A lot."

"I've missed you, too," she replied. She traced the line of his eyebrow with one finger. "Mitch?"

Mitch was busy absorbing every nuance of her face into his soul. "What, Jamie?"

"Those lessons I told you about. Remember? Lessons in loving?"

His brow puckered in a frown. "Yeah. What about them?"

"I'd like to start now, if you don't mind."

Mitch smiled, the sexy smile that turned her heart upside down. "No," he said, pulling her tighter against him, "I don't mind at all."

Epilogue

The spring sun beat down on Jamie's shoulders, which were bare except for the thin straps of her sundress. Sam, Leah and the boys were on her right, and Karen and Ian stood beside Mitch. All of them were yelling at the top of their lungs. The spring Special Olympics were well under way, and Chris and five other boys had just sprung from the starting blocks.

"Run, Chris!" Jamie yelled, jumping up and down beside her husband of a little over four weeks. Jamie and Mitch's marriage had been a month filled with struggle and love, fights and laughter. A month of learning to live with each other's quirks and foibles. A month of learning how to be a wife and mother as well as parish supervisor. A month of learning to be a husband and father as well as a businessman. It had been a month of lessons not only in learning to love, but also in learning what love really was and how many facets there were to it. It was a month Jamie wouldn't have traded for anything.

Chris, legs and arms pumping the way Mitch had shown him, passed one of the two boys still ahead of him. They were nearing the finish line.

"C'mon, Chris! You can do it!" Mitch yelled in typical fatherly fashion.

As if he heard Mitch above the roar of the crowd, Chris tucked in his chin and dug in his heels. He drew even with the boy in first place, and just before they reached the ribbon, Chris sprinted ahead.

"All right!" Jamie cried, bouncing up and down like a cork on water.

"Yeah!" Mitch yelled, his fist raised in a sign of victory. He grabbed Jamie and whirled her around in a giddy victory dance. "Not bad for only a month of training, huh?" he said with an arrogant, pleased-as-punch grin.

"Not bad," Jamie agreed. "Now, aren't you glad you let him run?"

Mitch's grin was sexy and sweet. "Yeah. I guess. But I'm glad you lost the bet, or I might still be chasing you."

"Doubtful, Mr. Bishop. Extremely doubtful," she said, leaning back in the circle of his arms and smiling up at him, her face glowing with happiness.

Mitch bent and kissed her, marveling as always at just how giving she was.

A few feet away, television cameras were capturing the kiss for the six o'clock news. Chris jogged up and stood looking at them, his hands on his hips and a disgusted look on his face.

"Hey, sport," the newscaster said, cocking his thumb at Mitch and Jamie much the way Chris often did. "What d'ya think of that?"

Chris shook his head and turned down the corners of his mouth. "Yucky!"

*   *   *   *   *

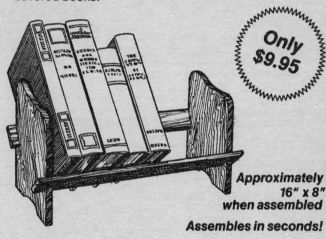

Silhouette Special Edition

COMING NEXT MONTH

#421 NO ROOM FOR DOUBT—Tracy Sinclair
No job too small or too difficult, Stacey Marlowe's ad boasted. But then she hadn't considered the demands her first customer would make. Shady Sean Garrison wanted—of all things!—her trust.

#422 INTREPID HEART—Anne Lacey
Trent Davidson would forever be a hero to Vanessa Hamilton. After all, he'd twice saved her life. But how could Trent settle for Vanessa's childlike adoration when he needed her womanly love?

#423 HIGH BID—Carole Halston
Katie Gamble was thrilled when fellow building contractor Louis McIntyre reentered her life. But Louis's gentle deception—and uneasy memories of a night long ago—threatened their bid for a future together.

#424 LOVE LYRICS—Mary Curtis
Ambitious lyricist Ashley Grainger lived and breathed Broadway, while her former fiancé, conservative lawyer Zachary Jordan, was Boston born and bred. Despite their renewed duet of passion, could they possibly find a lasting harmony?

#425 SAFE HARBOR—Sherryl Woods
When sexy neighbor Drew Landry filed a complaint about Tina Harrington's unorthodox household, they battled it out in the boardroom . . . and the bedroom . . . even as they longed for sweet compromise.

#426 LAST CHANCE CAFE—Curtiss Ann Matlock
Rancher Wade Wolcott wanted no part of Ellie McGrew's struggle to build a new life for her daughters. But the lovely, unassuming widow bought the farm next door, waited tables in his diner—and somehow crept into his heart.

AVAILABLE THIS MONTH:

#415 TIME AFTER TIME
Billie Green

#416 FOOLS RUSH IN
Ginna Gray

#417 WHITE NIGHTS
Dee Norman

#418 TORN ASUNDER
Celeste Hamilton

#419 SUMMER RAIN
Lisa Jackson

#420 LESSONS IN LOVING
Bay Matthews